LS65

Billy Morris

ISBN: 9798858652922

Print Edition

The author can be contacted at
BM.Author@outlook.com

Billy Morris was born in Leeds, Yorkshire in 1966. He left Leeds in the late 1990's and has lived and worked in Europe and USA. He now lives mainly in South-East Asia. He wrote his first book 'Bournemouth 90' in 2021, the sequel 'LS92' was published in 2022. His third book 'Birdsong on Holbeck Moor' was published in October 2022.

Acknowledgments

My thanks to the following people for their assistance in my research for this book. I was born in the mid-sixties so had no first-hand knowledge of the city of Leeds at the time and therefore relied on the memories of those who were around then, and were able to provide information and anecdotes covering Leeds United, Mods and scooters, clubs and coffee bars, music, drugs and the general life of a teenager in 1965. I hope I've managed to achieve an accurate representation of the city and the time.

Thank you all- David Wilson, David Dean, Mike Nutter, Raymond Diamond, Alan Swain, Helen Milton, Dave Cocker, Pam Varley Dacosta. Special thanks to ex-BG Club DJ General Justice.

Accents, Dialects and Pronunciation

LS65 is set in Leeds, a city in West Yorkshire in the North of England. The Leeds accent could generally be described as 'Yorkshire' but is quite distinct, and is easily identifiable when compared to speech in other parts of the county. Even different areas of the city have their own distinct dialects.

People in Leeds have a tendency to miss out letters, join words together and speak quite quickly. It's not an exaggeration to say that a conversation between Leeds folk could sound like a foreign language when compared to 'BBC English.'

Including dialogue exactly as it would most likely be spoken, would therefore make this book unreadable for many people. However, there are certain fundamental elements of the Leeds accent which I felt needed to be reflected, in order to maintain a level of authenticity in the characters' speech. The following substitutions have therefore been made throughout the book- -

The most obvious is the dropping of the word 'the' before a noun. In Leeds 'the' will be replaced by what linguists call a glottal stop. Execution of this element of the Leeds accent is generally difficult for a non-Yorkshire native. Actors on TV and in films usually get it wrong by either missing out 'the' entirely, or pronouncing a 't' in its place. As a Leeds speaker, I can't even explain how to execute a glottal stop. Google tells me it's achieved by rapidly closing the vocal chords. I've no idea how you do that. If you want to hear an example, I suggest you listen to an interview with David Batty or Kalvin Phillips. They're both experts. In the book, a glottal stop to replace 'the' is denoted by an apostrophe (').

"We're going to the pub' would therefore become "We're off to 'pub".

Owt, Nowt and Summat – The words anything, nothing and something will usually be replaced by owt, nowt and summat by a native Leeds speaker. The pronunciation of these words is open to some debate, but based on my own experience, I would say that owt is pronounced 'oat' and nowt is pronounced 'note', although I am aware that in some outlying parts of the city, both words would rhyme with 'shout'. Summat is universally pronounced 'summert'.

I recognise it may be confusing to include speech patterns which are unrecognisable beyond the boundaries of West Yorkshire, but I felt that dialect would become unrealistic in the context of the story without at least including these substitutions. I hope this doesn't impact on your enjoyment of the book.

Glasgow, January 1965

The monster was sat on the bench, where he always sat. Round the corner, behind the rubbish bins, in a small brick courtyard which offered some protection from the icy January winds which blew in off the Clyde. The monster knew that on the rare occasions there was a break in the grey cloud cover, a narrow shaft of weak sunlight would illuminate this bleak square for a fleeting moment. So now the monster sat, eyes closed and face tilted upwards, enjoying the unfamiliar sensation of warm, natural light on his face, not noticing as the young man approached across the empty exercise yard.

The young man clutched the pencil in his right hand, concealed in the pocket of his overalls, slowly increasing the pressure on the sharp lead tip with his thumb until he felt the sticky warmth of blood spread across his palm. Aware of the sound of the gravel shifting beneath his feet, he expected the monster to turn to face him, look into his eyes and realise that they were his own, then stand and smile nervously, unsure of what to say.

He'd played out the scene a thousand times in the days since he'd made his decision during art association. Since he'd turned away from the easel with the drawing of a crow that had turned into a bad peacock. Since he'd taken the roll of tape from his pocket and wrapped it around the pencil tip, then shrouded it in newspaper. Since he'd asked that wee cunt Mr. Tate if he could go for a piss, then crouched in the cubicle to slowly shove the pencil up his arse, then walked back into class like a tin soldier.

He'd played out the scene a thousand times of how the monster would see him for the first time. How he'd not be scared anymore. How the monster would cry and

1

plead for mercy. How he'd tell him the rule. No fucking prisoners.

But now, standing a few feet away, looking down at the leathery skin, tinted orange in the winter sunlight, the baggy overalls hanging from a skinny frame, the knuckles with the tattooed dots that once broke his nose, he realised that the monster was already dead. He'd rehearsed what to say, gone over the words in his head a thousand times, but now he knew that there was no point.

The monster looked up as the boy's shadow stole the sunlight, and recognition fought a losing battle with confusion in his watery eyes. He glanced left towards the young man's right hand but his arms remained by his side as the sharp tip of the pencil penetrated the side of his neck. The young man stepped away as the monster stood and took two steps forward with blood spraying through his fingers, before sinking to his knees. Their eyes met and the monster's lips quivered, tears in his eyes, trying to understand. Why?

The young man wiped the pencil on the leg of his overalls and smiled. *Not scared of the monster anymore.*

Chapter 1

Wednesday, 10 March 1965

The kids got on the train when it stopped at Harrogate. Three posh schoolboys in blazers and caps entered the compartment where he'd spent the last three hours, eyes closed, inhaling the parma-violet scent from the middle-aged woman who'd sat facing him since Carlisle. Sniggering and jostling, the boys immediately slid open the window and then left it ajar when they got off at Pannal. Alan Connolly opened one eye as the boys stepped clumsily over his outstretched legs, resisting the urge to lift his foot and smash it into the last kid's skinny arse, to send him spinning into the aisle.

The chill late winter air filled the compartment and the middle aged woman sniffed and tutted, but the cold breeze began to stir Alan from his torpid state, so the window stayed open. The temperature quickly dipped as green fields were replaced by scattered stone farm buildings, then white painted pre-war semis, then rows of red brick terraces. The train rattled across a viaduct, and Alan Connolly turned to his left to see the spires and domes and high-rise concrete towers of Leeds, Yorkshire, England. His first glimpse of a city outside Scotland. His new home, the place he would pursue his destiny, build his empire. *A man with a plan. No fucking prisoners.*

He retrieved the blue BOAC holdall from the overhead rack and pulled on his olive-green, ex-US Army parka, smiled and muttered a goodbye to the woman he'd ignored for two hours, and was already turning the rusted door-handle before the train slowed to a halt beside a brown sign with white lettering. 'Leeds Central'.

Alan Connolly felt the knot in his stomach tighten and the electrical charge in his brain surge. *Your brain is just wired wrong. Everyone has voices in their head but it seems yours are too loud to ignore.*

That's what the doctor at Larchgrove had said, and he enjoyed that feeling, that surging adrenaline current which powered his thoughts and directed his actions.

He felt the gritty deposits in his teeth, and his eyes itched from the sooty smoke which had filled the carriage as the train passed through a tunnel a few miles outside Leeds. He glanced down and spotted a dark smudge on his white cycling shirt.

"Shite. Wee bastards." He now regretted not giving the schoolboys something to remember him by. He stepped onto the platform and looked up at an iron latticed roof with moss-stained glass panels casting a dull green light across the blackened brickwork of the station buildings. Passing a scuffed brown door with white lettering saying Waiting Room, he spotted a large rectangular mirror covering one wall and pushed open the door.

The room smelt of a cold, damp Yorkshire winter and a hundred years of tobacco, and an elderly couple sat in silence, the man absent-mindedly tapping the handle of a large maroon suitcase.

Moving towards the mirror, Alan peered at his own reflection. He licked the back of his index finger and rubbed it beneath his eye to remove a fleck of soot. He then spat on the sleeve of his parka and used it to rub at the dark smudge on his cycling shirt. He bent to straighten the Levi's which he'd spent two hours shrinking to fit, in a tub at the Govanhill public bath-house. He then used his thumb to remove a fleck of mud from the shoes he'd liberated from the Hampden Bowl in Sommerville Drive. He had contemplated wearing his new suit for the journey - an Italian 'bum freezer' jacket with a 16-inch centre vent, but was glad now he'd opted for the casual look, otherwise his first day in England would have been spent looking for a dry cleaner.

He straightened up and caught the eye of the old woman in the mirror and she quickly looked away. He tilted his head in order to check the half parting in his hair, back-combed over the crown just like Steve Marriott's.

"You look grand lad." He turned and the old man smiled at him.

Alan Connolly nodded to the old man and pulled open the door. He turned right past the ladies waiting room and paused before another brown sign with white letters spelling 'Way Out'. He put his hands into the front pockets of his Levi's, careful to leave the thumbs sticking out. He straightened his back and set off walking with short steps, swaying his shoulders as he moved in an exaggerated swagger. The Mod walk. Like his clothes, his hair, his demeanour, the way he walked told the world exactly who he was. What he was. The steady hum of electricity in his brain increasing in intensity. *I can go anywhere, where I choose.*

He exited the station onto a cobbled parking area, sloping down towards an imposing, six storey building with 'Great Northern Hotel' displayed in gold letters on its red brick frontage. He paused and placed his holdall on the damp cobbles, slowly tugging the zip of his parka upwards in response to a chill wind which rippled his cycling shirt. He scanned the car park and the road beyond, watching a two-tone green bus rumbling past, its exhaust spewing black smoke.

"Post! Eeen Post!" The vendor had a gaunt face the colour of mustard and a hand rolled cigarette in the corner of his mouth. He stood alongside a stand with a hand written headline 'Peacock Back for United Cup Clash.' Alan Connolly approached, fumbling in his parka pocket to retrieve two penny pieces and handed them over to the man, who folded a broadsheet with print-blackened hands and silently thrust it towards him.

Alan Connolly took a deep breath and inhaled a cocktail of coal smoke and exhaust fumes. England smelt the same as Scotland. It felt as cold and the people looked the same, though the dark Yorkshire stone and soot-stained red brick lent an oppressive air to the scene. A flutter of apprehension appeared without warning in his stomach and he fought hard to dispel it as he unfolded the newspaper and looked at the headline.

Train Raid Hunt in Millionaires Resort - 'Wilson, Buster and Co seen sunbathing.' Montevideo, Uruguay -Police at Punta del Este, the main beach resort of the country, were on patrol today with orders to watch for Charles Wilson and three men Scotland Yard think may be able to assist their investigation into the Great Train Robbery. Interpol believe the fugitives entered the country last week using false passports.

Alan smiled. It was nearly two years since the robbery and the police were no nearer catching the gang or recovering the £2 million haul. A proper job, planned to perfection and executed well. Something to aspire to. *A man with a plan.*

The double headlights of a black Ford Zodiac blinked at the far end of the car park in the shadow of the hotel. Alan Connolly picked up his bag and set off across the wet cobbles, smiling as he spotted his brother's gap-toothed grin behind the steering wheel. Alongside him sat an older man, early thirties, unsmiling beneath a trilby hat.

He'd thought about this moment a thousand times while he was locked up in Larchgrove and Barlinnie. Meeting Keith again after five years had kept him going through the long days in bang-up, the night-terrors and beatings, the sodomy and suicides. He'd wondered if his brother would embrace him. Then no, not Keith. They'd never been a hugging type of family. Maybe a firm handshake. Meeting his younger brother, man to man for the first time.

"Alright wee man. Get yourself in." Keith Connolly nodded towards the backseat through the open car window and Alan tugged open the door and climbed in to sit alongside a large box bearing a photo of a child in a dalek suit.

"Lost your false teeth again?" He'd wondered what his first words would be and surprised himself with a reference to the dentistry trauma inflicted by a Barrowlands doorman on Keith's 18th birthday.

"Ach, fucking broke the bastards didn't I?" Keith turned in his seat and rolled his top lip back to reveal his gums. "You alright anyway?"

"Aye, I'm alright. What's this? You doing fancy dress?" Alan tapped the box beside him.

"This is Terry. That's for Max, his wee boy. A gift from one of our...clients." Keith tilted his head towards the passenger seat and the older man turned and extended his hand.

"Nice to meet you, your brother's told me a lot about you."

Alan gripped the man's hand firmly and met his gaze.

"Aye, likewise." As soon as he'd said it, he wished he hadn't. *Fucking idiot. Think before you speak.*

The electricity in his head crackled and the knot of apprehension in his stomach tightened. He was wondering whether he should say something else, but the man released his hand and smiled and nodded towards him.

"Going camping are you?"

"Erm...what?" Alan followed Terry's gaze down towards his parka.

"Fucking rent-a-tent is it?" Terry Jackson smirked and Keith Connolly laughed out loud and turned the ignition key, and the Zodiac's 1700cc engine sprang to life. In the backseat, Alan Connolly felt his face redden and the knot in his stomach tightened more. His brother's laughter caused his eyes to prickle and his mouth to dry up, so he was unable to speak. Five long years he'd waited for this moment, and here was some fucking stranger disrespecting him in front of Keith, belittling him, spoiling everything. *It's not meant to be like this.*

"Let's get you to your new gaff then brother, and we can have a proper catch-up." Keith called over his shoulder as he pulled the car onto the main road and turned right in front of the Great Northern Hotel.

Alan Connolly bit his lip and breathed heavily through his nostrils as the car navigated a roundabout with a statue of a knight on horseback, facing the blackened, smoke-tainted frontage of the Queens Hotel. He felt the switch flick in his head and the electrical charge fizzed into life as the voices got louder. He unzipped his parka and reached inside, feeling for the pocket he'd stitched into the lining, the cold steel of the bayonet held within.

He stared hard at the back of the head of the man in the passenger seat and felt his heart rate begin to slow, his breath becoming calmer as he imagined showing this wanker Terry exactly who he was. What he was. *I'm a man with a plan. You'll be working for me within a year, Terry Jackson. And the world will know the name, Alan Connolly. Tick Tock.*

Chapter 2

"Hitler was going to use these flats as his northern headquarters If he'd won the war." Keith Connolly pulled back the net curtains and peered through the drizzle-flecked window pane at two men pushing an Austin 1100 into the Eastgate roundabout petrol station. "Seventh floor too, so no noise from above and the lift usually works. Not bad for your first bachelor pad eh?"

"I thought I might have been staying with you, you know, maybe to start with anyway..." Alan Connolly joined his brother at the window.

"Listen mate, you'll need your own space once you start entertaining." Keith turned and winked.

"Entertaining?"

"The ladies, brother. You'll be fighting them off, believe me."

Alan laughed nervously and turned away, flopping down onto a threadbare maroon settee in the corner of the room.

"Chance would be a fine thing."

Keith joined him on the couch. "No joke. The line of work you're going to be in, you'll have the pick of the lassies. Believe me, I know from experience. Leeds is the land of opportunity!" He squeezed his brother's knee.

"I'll believe it when I see it. So go on, what's the plan?"

Keith stood up and walked into a small adjoining kitchen and lit the hob with his lighter.

"Tea? Not sure there's any milk though."

"Nah, you're okay."

Keith filled a kettle and placed it on the hob, then leaned on the kitchen door frame to address his brother.

"You'll be doing what I was, before I got promoted."

"So you'll be my boss?"

"Not exactly, it's what you might call a fluid management structure. But we all work for the same bloke, Clive Donovan."

"What's he do then, this Donovan?"

Keith turned back into the kitchen in response to a shrill whistle from the kettle and returned holding a steaming mug.

"A better question would be what doesn't he do." Keith smiled. "This flat is one of his. So is the one I live in, over in the next block. He owns hundreds of properties. He also has what I'll refer to as an interesting mix of business ventures."

"Business ventures like what?" Alan Connolly pulled himself upright on the couch. Clive Donovan sounded like the sort of person he could learn from. *A man with a plan.*

"Let's just say, he can get hold of just about anything anyone could ever want to buy. He also owns a large security company, which is the arm of the business we work in. He runs all the bouncers at the pubs and clubs. Basically we ensure the safety and wellbeing of more or less every business in Leeds city centre."

"Safety? What like store detectives?"

"Not really. More prevention of crime. Pubs getting smashed up, shops getting set on fire, that type of thing."

"Does that happen much here then? It sounds worse than Glasgow."

Keith Connolly sniffed and took a sip from his mug. "It only tends to happen to businesses that decline to pay for our services, if you get what I mean..."

Alan nodded and smiled. "Got you...so where do I fit in?"

Keith joined him back on the settee. "As I said, Mr Donovan can source virtually any product which someone may want to buy. And we know what your lot want to buy, don't we Al?"

"My lot?"

"Mods. And Rockers too. What you lot want to buy is something to keep you dancing all night."

"Pills..."

"Correct. Pills. And lots of them. We control the entire supply in Leeds. Mr Donovan's doormen ensure we have free rein in the pubs and clubs, but the biggest market is the coffee bars, the Del Rio, El Toro, the Conca d'Ora, places where the younger mods go. I'm twenty five now, too old to be hanging out in those places, and I've got bigger fish to fry. We have a few lads working the coffee bars and doing some low level protection stuff, but they're disorganised and a bit daft if I'm honest. Mr Donovan needs someone to whip them into shape and get them functioning as a proper team. I told him you'd be up for it?"

"You told him about me?" *The switch flicked and the electricity flashed and crackled in his head.*

"Yeah. Well, not everything, just that you were relocating and looking for a new opportunity. He said that if I vouched for you then he was happy to give you a chance."

"Yeah, great. That's really great. Thanks Keith. I won't let you down..."

His sentence was cut short as Keith Connolly rose from the couch and walked back to stare out of the window.

"So, tell me what happened..."

"What happened with what?"

"Bridget wrote and said you were out, that you were going to keep your head down and get a job. Next I heard, you were the most wanted man in the whole of fucking Scotland."

Alan Connolly inhaled deeply and sank back onto the couch with his hands behind his head, staring at the cracked plaster of the ceiling. *Switch flicked, electricity surging, current buzzing in his head, into his veins.*

"I had a job to do."

"A job? Running with a team isn't a job Alan. It's fucking pointless when there's no money in it. You'd just done nearly three years inside." Keith shook his head and retreated into the kitchen where his muttered comments were obscured by the running of the tap.

"It wasn't just about the Cumbie. It was personal." *Police sirens, sweat and tobacco, blades and Buckfast flashing through his mind.*

"What's that?" Keith re-appeared in the kitchen doorway.

"It was nothing to do with the Young Cumbie. I hadn't even seen any of the boys since I'd got out. But this kid Benny from the Shamrocks, he was the one who'd chibbed Tam up at the Green. Everyone knew it. He didn't shut up about it while I was away. I couldn't just let that go." *Electrical charge coursing through his veins. Blood on his hands.*

13

"So you hit the fucker with an axe..."

"He killed my best pal Keith. He was laughing about it. I got word to him through Molloy that I wanted a square go, but he didn't show, the fucking coward. Then I heard he was in the snooker club on Great George Street, so I went to see him."

"With a fucking axe..."

"Yeah well, turned out I needed it. Him and his two pals all pulled razors on me. I had to fight my way out.

"Did his arm actually come right off then?" Keith seemed to be trying to suppress a half smile now.

"He was laying across the table, it was sort of hanging off. Looked fucking great on the green under the lights..." *Blood on his hands.*

"Jesus Christ Alan. What the fuck are we going to do with you?" Keith was laughing now, and Alan felt a weight lift from his shoulders.

"You need to learn to use your head from now on. Don't get nicked for anything stupid. The coppers down here are cunts, especially the CID. Big Red Holmes, Moose Walker, Buffer Brailsford, proper hard bastards. Stay out of their way and give them a different name if you get lifted, tell them you're under sixteen to stop them taking your prints."

Alan nodded as Keith slumped on the couch beside him. It felt good to have his big brother alongside him again. Keith's approval meant everything. Alan swallowed and his mouth felt dry. *Tell him now. Don't spoil the moment. Tell him now.*

"There's something else."

"Yeah?" Keith didn't turn to face him, carried on looking at his own feet, but his voice betrayed an apprehension at what his brother was about to say.

"Yeah." A momentary silence was broken as Alan took a deep breath, stood, and walked to the window, staring out towards the central bus station, grey sky turning black, focusing on slowing his breathing, unplugging the electrical current.

"It's about Barlinnie."

Chapter 3

"The Bar-L. Fuck me Alan. Bridget never said."

"Aye, they moved me from Larchgrove when I hit eighteen. Bridget didn't know. No one did." He closed one eye, lining up a slow moving raindrop on the window pane with a car pulling out of Millgarth police station, pulling an imaginary trigger. *Bang. You're dead.*

"Barlinnie at eighteen. That's tough. Fucking hell Alan." Keith had taken a packet of Embassy from his jacket pocket and flicked his lighter three times before the cigarette end glowed orange.

"I was alright. Got padded up with an old pal of yours..."

"Aye? I know plenty in there." Keith narrowed his eyes as he drew on the cigarette.

"Frankie Fields."

Keith scowled and shook his head.

"He's a cunt, no mistake."

"Aye well, he remembered me somehow, so he looked after me when I first got in, kept the chicken-hawks away, you know, showed me what's what, but you're right. He is a cunt." Alan turned back to face his brother who shuffled forward on the settee, his face momentarily lost in cigarette smoke. *Don't spoil the moment. Tell him now.*

Alan took a deep breath and exhaled loudly before continuing.

"Did you know that's where he is?"

Keith lowered the cigarette and looked across at his brother.

"Where who is?.....Da'?"

Alan turned to look out of the window. "Aye. Da'"

"I thought he was in Greenock...but I heard...oh fuck." Keith's mouth fell open and he lifted his hands and rubbed at his temples.

"Oh fuck, Alan, no. That wasn't you?"

"What did you hear?" *Electricity surging through his mind, into his veins. Tell him what you are. Who you are.*

"That he'd been stabbed. He was in the hospital. They didn't think he'd make it so they contacted Bridget. What the fuck...that was you? Jesus Christ Alan." Keith slumped forward, his head buried in his hands.

"Aye. I fucked it up though. Stuck him in the neck with a pencil. Blood squirted everywhere, I thought I'd got the main vein. Can't believe they managed to save the bastard." *Blood on his hands. No fucking prisoners.*

"But how...how did you know it was him? How come they didn't pinch you for it?" Keith was standing now, pacing the floor, hands rubbing at his temples.

"I heard his voice. I can never forget that voice. I heard him speak and I remembered. I was nine years old last time I saw him, but I recognised him straight away. He looked older but I knew. He didn't know me though, so I bided my time. Stole a pencil from art class. He was on a different wing, but I knew where he always sat during association. I waited till I had my release date, then I just walked up to him one morning. He was sat on a bench. There was no one else nearby and he nodded at me, and I wondered if he knew it was me. He didn't though. I'd been planning what to say, hello Da' or that's for Ma or some shite like that, but in the end I couldn't speak. I just took the pencil out of my pocket and stuck it in his neck."

"For fuck's sake Alan..." Keith was shaking now and he voice cracked as he spoke.

"Blood squirted out. Went all over. He fell off the bench and I walked away. I was expecting sirens to go off and everything but there was nothing. The whistle went and we all went back to the cells. I washed my hands under a tap in the yard, but there were a few bits I missed. I was shaking a bit too when I got back to the cell..."

"Frankie?"

"Aye, I told him what had happened. He took the pencil, said he'd get rid of it. Helped me clean my gear. Then it all went quiet. People talked about it a bit, but there's chibbings every week in there, so it was no big deal. And there's loads called Connolly so no one ever connected me to Da'. I got out two weeks later."

"Fucking hell Alan. So what's the score with Fields?" Keith took another cigarette from the packet and lit it, tip to tip.

"Said I owed him. For looking after me, then covering up about Da'. He gets out next month. He's got a girl over in Ireland. Says he's going to make a new start there. I have to meet him when he's out."

Keith clenched his fists and shook his head.

"Aye, that sounds about right for him. How much does he want?"

"Two hundred quid. He's kept the pencil and says if I don't pay he'll hand that to the police and also tell them that me and dad are related. Once they find that out and realise that he's in for killing my Ma', then it's pretty obvious I did it. What with the Benny thing too, they're going to be coming for me. "

"Ahhh, fuck!" Keith slumped back on the settee and stared at the ceiling. "I haven't got that kind of money to lend you."

"There's another thing..." Alan turned back to look out of the window. "I told him you were down here, so when I don't show with his cash and I'm nowhere to be found in Glasgow, he's going to tell them where to look."

"Fucking brilliant." Keith looked at his shoes and shook his head. " For fuck's sake Alan, why did you do it? Why risk getting banged up for life for that?"

Alan pressed his forehead to the window, enjoying the feel of the cold glass on his warm skin. *Because of who I am. Wired wrong. Voices too loud to ignore.*

"He killed our Ma' Keith, killed our Ma, tried to kill me after years of beating us black and blue, and you ask fucking why?" Alan turned back to his brother, the anger flashing in his eyes, the thoughts racing in his head. *Do you see me for what I am now brother?*

"You were just a wee boy when it happened. You don't remember everything."

"Well fucking tell me then! Fucking tell me Keith, because no one has ever told me what really happened that day, not you or Bridget or June or Maggie or Claire...no one has ever told me why he tried to kill me, why he murdered our mother, why he tortured us, why we had to steal food to eat, why we slept under coats in a bedroom with moss growing on the walls...so you go ahead and fucking tell me Keith!" *Electricity surging, white light flashing bright behind his eyes.*

Keith stood up and walked to the window to stand alongside his brother. "Aye he was a bastard. It wasn't all him though...Ma had her own problems. Big problems. When I was a wee boy, Bridget more or less raised me. Then it was the same with you. I used to change your shitey nappy, bath you. I was fucking seven years old. That wasn't down to the old man."

"So she was a drunk, a shit mother. But she loved us, she must have, she died saving my fucking life remember? Stopped that bastard drowning me and took a knife blade for it." Alan blinked back tears, turning his face away from his brother, looking beyond the bus station to a herd of forlorn cattle being walked in a funerary procession from Marsh Lane station to the abattoir on New York Street.

"Believe me, she wasn't perfect. You were eight when she died, you were too young to understand." Keith slowly raised his hand and Alan flinched, anticipating a contact which never came.

"The war ruined Da' that's what they all said. He had an apprenticeship at Fairfields, Ma had just had Bridget, they were all set up. Then the war started when he was twenty. Took away the best years of his life. Ma said he was never the same after his best mate died in his arms in Burma. That must have really affected him."

Keith realised his mistake as soon as he'd uttered the words. "I'm sorry Al. I forgot about Tam. I wasn't thinking. This is all just a shock, that's all."

Alan shook his head, still facing away, then held out his hand and Keith passed him the cigarette.

"My only regret is not killing the bastard, doing to him what he did to our Ma. And if I get another chance, I won't fuck it up again believe me."

The room fell silent, Alan staring at the steady flow of black and grey cars passing in front of Millgarth police station heading towards Eastgate, not responding to the sound of his brother pacing behind him.

"So what will you do? About Fields?"

"I reckon I've got two choices." Alan spoke slowly and quietly causing Keith to pause. "Either I meet up with him next month and kill the fucker..."

"For fuck's sake Alan, he's connected, he works for Borradale, you can't just go round killing folk, Jesus Christ..."

"Or..."Alan turned to face his brother. "Option two, I get my head down and start grafting hard and you help me find a way to earn the money."

"Two hundred quid in a month? How the fuck are we going to do that?"

Alan stared out at the car park and the drizzle, the black sky turning grey.

"Land of opportunity you said wasn't it? Well, I'm not down here for a wee holiday brother. They ran some classes in Larchgrove, to set us up for life outside. Load of shite really, but the old guy who ran it used to come up with these sayings that were pretty good. One of them was 'Success is the offspring of ideas and bravery', and I thought, aye, I like that, because I've got fucking loads of both those things. Tons of ideas and I'm not scared of anything. I'm a man with a plan and I'm here to make some serious money...so when do I start?"

Chapter 4

Thursday 11 March 1965

Come Back Soon Cry to Beatles - Beatlemania hit London airport again today as over 2000 teenagers hung precariously over the airport's viewing galleries, screaming for the group. The Beatles were off to Austria to continue location work on their second film. As the BEA Vanguard airliner lifted slowly from the runway, cries of 'Please come home soon!' drifted from the roof gardens.

'Del Rio Coffee Bar.' Alan Connolly read the hand painted sign aloud as he followed his brother up the cobbled sidestreet in the looming shadow of Mill Hill Chapel. Keith pushed open the glass door and led the way down a short flight of stairs.

"Two frothy coffees please Luigi." Keith called to a dark haired man behind the counter who waved in acknowledgement. A juke box played 'The In Crowd' by Dobie Gray and the Magic City pinball machine popped and buzzed and rattled in response to the frenzied flipper fingers of a large youth in a sheepskin coat.

Keith nodded to direct his brother towards a corner table where a youth in a Prince of Wales check suit jacket and another in a blue cardigan and Fred Perry polo shirt turned to greet them. An olive green parka was hung on the back of each of their wooden seats.

"Norman, Wesley, this is my brother Alan. He's going to be working with you boys from now on."

The youths muttered their acknowledgements but neither extended a hand in greeting as the brothers joined them at the table.

"Scotty is the other lad you'll be working with. He'll be here soon."

Alan assessed the youths as Norman began to tell his brother about a missed collection at a greengrocer's stall in the open market.

Wesley was in his late teens, dark greasy hair with a dog-legged parting, brushed left to right. He wore a lambswool cardigan which had clearly been washed too often and now suffered from visible bobbling. The top button on his Fred Perry was undone, causing the collar to ripple untidily. The transition to daily shaving had clearly not yet been made and consequently a wispy shadow of moustache tainted his upper lip.

Norman's suit jacket was clearly off the peg, not made to measure, three button with rounded lapels, though it had a nice butterfly cuff. It could have looked good with a quality shirt, a Peter England or Ben Sherman, but Norman's was cheap and white from the market, Dyloned to a pastel shade, with a Bond Street collar attached. His hair was cut in the type of spikey razor style which had been popular in early 64.

 In short, these boys were a fucking shambles, third class tickets, and Alan began to feel annoyed by their sloppiness. He suddenly became aware that the conversation around the table had paused and everyone was looking at him.

"You up for it then brother?" Keith was looking at him as he spooned sugar into his coffee.

"Sorry, what's that, I was miles away for a minute." Alan felt his face redden as the others laughed.

"Leeds beat Crystal Palace in the cup last night. Wesley here is a big fan. He's screwing a lassie from the ticket office so all the lads are relying on him for semi-final tickets. You'll be up for it if he gets some won't you?"

"She helped us out for Shrewsbury in 'last round but this is different, it'll be harder for her to slip some aside for this one. They're only giving us twenty one thousand for Hillsborough and we're averaging forty one thousand at home. Man Utd are getting about thirty thousand." Wesley puffed out his cheeks and shook his head at the injustice being inflicted upon his team by the corrupt Football Association.

Alan had never been overly interested in football, but most of the Gorbals Young Cumbie were big Celtic fans and the close proximity of Protestant rivals such as the Ibrox Tongs and the Scotstoun Fleet had meant there was always an opportunity for some sectarian, football related violence, which suited him just fine.

"We've got some great Scottish players in 'team." Wesley grinned enthusiastically, "Billy Bremner, Bobby Collins, Jim Storrie..."

"Willie Bell in defence too." Norman chipped in, "and some cracking prospects in 'juniors and reserves. Edwin Gray and Peter Lorimer are our age, you'll probably see them at 'Arcade Mecca."

"Aye, count me in. Is the Mecca the best dance hall then?"

"The Key Hole Club upstairs mostly play chart stuff so we don't bother going, but the coffee bar downstairs has a good lunchtime scene. The BG in White Horse Yard, Ioannas next to 'station, the all-nighter at 'Three Coins, they all play some good music."

"You missed out 'best place..." Norman tipped the spilt tea from his saucer into his cup.

"Here we go..." Smiled Wesley.

"The American bar on Wellington Street has 'best juke box in Leeds," Norman continued. "Proper Blues and Soul stuff that you don't hear anywhere else. Certainly no chart shit."

"Norman is an American music expert. Hates The Who, Small Faces, Stones..."

"What...you hate the Stones and you call yourself a Mod?" Alan couldn't let that go unchallenged. Jagger was one of the few people he admired. His style, his simmering aggression and raw sexuality, his fuck-you attitude. To Alan, Mick Jagger epitomised what it meant to be a Mod.

"The Stones aren't Mods, they're just dressed-up art students who've stolen and massacred classics by proper artists like Muddy Waters, Chuck Berry and Ben E King. They're a bloody disgrace." Alan couldn't believe what he was hearing, and Keith and Wesley dissolved into laughter as Norman warmed to his theme.

"Come with me to 'American bar Alan, and I'll put some proper music on 'juke box for you, Eddie Jefferson, Jimmy Witherspoon, Jimmy Reed..."

"Spencer Davies Group..." Wesley smirked as he took a sip of his tea.

"Fucking Spencer Davies. Shit. You'll be telling me the fucking Kinks are a mod band next."

"The Who...?" Keith was struggling to keep up with the conversation.

"Roger and Pete are actually proper faces, I'll give them that. Not sure about John though, and Keith doesn't know what he his. They're still playing manufactured music though. They're a pop band. Georgie Fame is more of a mod than The Who."

"Norman rides out to 'Sun Inn on 'way to Harrogate to buy records from a couple of black lads who work at the US base out there." Wesley was tapping his temple to indicate what he thought of his friend's musical obsession. "Tell him what you paid for that record the other week."

"You Better Move on, by Arthur Alexander, cost me nearly a week's wages." Norman looked pleased with his purchase, but the rest of the table were convulsed by laughter.

"A week's wages for a single?" Keith was shaking his head, when a youth in a parka appeared on the stairs and shouted a greeting.

"That's Scotty. And he's got a surprise for you Alan." Keith stood and the group picked up their parkas and followed him up the steps and out of the door onto Basinghall Street, where the young man was hauling a blue Lambretta onto its centre-stand alongside two other scooters parked opposite the café.

"You took the fly-screen off then?" The young man was rubbing at an oily smudge on the chrome wheel-trim and he stood up as the others gathered in a semi-circle around the scooter.

"Yeah, no one has a fly-screen now. There was too much stuff on it, it looked shit. Most lads are going for a simpler look now, so I got rid of a load of 'mirrors and lamps, just left a couple of spotlights either side of 'crash bar, and I've put yellow cellophane on them. They'll look good lit up. Two extra mirrors and I've chromed 'rear rack. I left 'Silver Lady mascot on too."

He handed the keys to Alan. "You must be Keith's brother. This is your welcome present."

"You what? This is for me...?" Alan felt his eyes moisten and struggled to stop his hands shaking with excitement as he stepped forward and took the keys. *I can go anywhere, where I choose.*

"It's a repossession. The kid who owned it borrowed the money off Mr.Donovan, but he's missed three week's worth of payments, so you can use it till he catches up. If he ever catches up."

"Fucking hell Keith, thanks, it's brilliant. What is it, a GS?" Alan straddled the scooter's white saddle and turned the key and the bike rattled into life.

"GT 200, it's a decent ride, probably 'best there is at 'moment aside from a TV. It'll do 65 at a push, I just got 58 out of it on York Road." Scotty stepped back to admire the scooter and flicked at a smudge on one of the headlamps.

"Scotty knows everything there is to know about scooters. Any problems, give him a shout." Keith circled the bike, giving the front wheel a half-hearted kick.

"I had 70 out of my Vespa on 'way to Scarborough in August." Norman spat on his palm and ran it the length of an aerial flying a squirrel tail on another parked scooter.

"Top speed on a 160 is sixty downhill if you're lucky, you lying bastard." Scotty laughed and shook his head.

"You didn't go down to the south coast last summer then? I heard that's where all the action was." Alan revved the engine of the Lambretta and the narrow street echoed to the metallic rattle.

"No, we usually go to Scarborough, but some of 'lads from 'Conc went to Skegness at August Bank Holiday and had a massive scrap with some rockers from Hull."

"What's the Conc?"

"La Conca d'Ora coffee bar round 'corner in Upper Mill Hill. You get loads of mods in there, good place for us selling. I hear you're going to be working with us?" Scotty raised his voice to be heard above the sputtering revs of the scooter engine and Alan turned off the ignition.

"Aye, looking forward to you boys showing me the ropes, telling me what's what round here..."

"Well Friday's a big day for collections round town. You can join the boys doing that today, then I'll see you back at my flat later, when you pick up the gear·for the weekend." Keith removed the car keys from his jacket pocket and turned and set off walking towards Boar Lane, calling over his shoulder as he went.

"Have a good day boys, and behave yourselves!"

Chapter 5

For three hours Alan Connolly remained silent. Silent, as the smell of cold blood in the stalls of Kirkgate market's butcher's row made him feel nauseous; Silent, as the dust-filled draper's shops made him cough; He bit his tongue as his new colleagues moaned about the wages which barely supplemented their unemployment benefit; He resisted the urge to comment on their ill-fitting clothes, their scuffed shoes and their badly styled hair; He yawned through Wesley's discussion of Albert Johanneson's shin injury ahead of Leeds United's upcoming trip to Fulham; rubbed his eyes as Scotty told them how Vespa had started adding 100MPH speedos to their scooters without even increasing the capacity of the engine; and sighed loudly as Norman explained how he'd had 'Nowhere to Run' by Martha and the Vandellas shipped from America, but it now wouldn't arrive until after the single was released in Britain. He quietly observed their amateurish attempts to appear threatening, to assert control, to persuade and cajole, to achieve their goals. But then at 3.28 in Morrison's Hardware store on Kirkgate, Alan Connolly could remain silent no more.

"No."

It was a single word, uttered by a man in his early fifties, wearing a neatly pressed brown overall and dark, horn-rimmed spectacles, and it caused Alan's colleagues to flinch. Norman and Wesley looked at each other, then Wesley nudged Scotty who hesitatingly stepped forward.

"What do you mean no, Malcolm?"

"I mean I've had enough." The shopkeeper removed his glasses and placed them slowly in the top pocket of his brown overall. "I've worked it out. Worked out how much I've paid you lot over the last eight years, and you know what..?" He folded his arms and waited for an answer as the three youths shuffled nervously.

"I've worked out that if I hadn't been tipping up three quid a week to you, or rather your boss, I could have bought this shop outright."

"Yeah, but Malcolm, what good would that be if something happened to 'shop, it got burn down or summat?" Scotty was flexing his knuckles, as Norman gently shoved him forward.

"If it caught fire, then I'd put the fucking fire out! If someone smashed the window, I'd board it up and replace it! And if any little cunts came into my shop trying to threaten me, I'd punch them on the nose and sling them out!" Malcolm Morrison's raised voice, purple face and bulging neck veins caused the boys to take a step back.

Malcolm Morrison had spent two years fighting the Japs in the jungles of Malaya. Chasing shadows in the jungle, wading through leach-infested swamps in torrential rain. The only Japanese soldiers he'd seen up close were dead ones. His war had consisted of multiple hours of uncomfortable boredom, punctuated by the sudden terror of sporadic and unexpected sniper fire.

He'd never seen a Japanese bayonet at close quarters until 3.28 on the 11th March 1965, in his Hardware shop on Kirkgate, when he felt one pressing into the soft flesh, less than an inch beneath his left eye.

Pushed backwards onto the counter, his back bent at an unnatural angle, Malcolm Morrison flinched as a salty rivulet of blood trickled down his cheek and reached his lips.

"You can put out a fire and board up a broken window, but how will a blind man find the correct thread of screw for a customer?" Malcolm's heart pounded as he looked along the long blade at the unsmiling young man who had stepped from behind the three thugs in his shop, brandishing the small sword.

"Could a man with no eyes cut a key do you think?" Alan Connolly stared down the blade into the small black eyes of the cowering shopkeeper. *Switch flicked, electrical current charged, power humming in his brain.*

"Please no...I'm sorry...I'll pay up, I promise." A hot, wet patch appeared in the crotch of Malcolm Morrison's grey slacks and a pool began to spread around his polished black brogues, as a slow tear trickled from his left eye to dilute the blood trickling down his cheek.

The blade pressed deeper into the skin beneath the eye socket and Alan could hear Norman's panicked breathing beside him. *Keep your head down. Don't get nicked for anything stupid.*

"Oh, you'll pay alright Malcolm. I tell you what though, you won't be paying three quid anymore. It's going to be four from now on. Is that alright Malcolm?"

"Yes, yes, I'll pay, I'm sorry."

Alan Connolly retracted the blade from Malcolm Morrison's eye socket and wiped it clean of blood on the shopkeeper's brown overall.

"Aye, you'll pay four quid a week from now on, and you'll thank me for sparing your eyes."

"Yes, yes, I will." Malcolm hauled himself upright and rested his hands on the counter.

"Go on then." Alan Connolly stepped forward, forcing Malcolm back over the counter again.

"Thank you...thank you."

"Thank you for what?" whispered Alan Conolly, his nose an inch from Malcolm's.

"Thank you for not taking my eyes, thank you." Malcolm's face crumpled and his tears and his blood fell into the pool of piss on the floor of the shop.

"You're very welcome Malcolm." Alan Connolly turned to the other lads and nodded towards the door, then turned once more and levelled the bayonet at the shaking man leaning on the counter.

"Oh and Malcolm, be sure to tell all your fellow shopkeepers and business owners about my visit today. Tell them that I'll be round to see them all very soon. My name is Alan. Alan Connolly. You be sure to remember that name as you're going to be hearing a lot of it from now on."

Chapter 6

Dark. Awake.

Wet on the blankets. Wet on the coats.

Hot and wet on his face.

Claire crying.

Ya dirty bastard you, ya've pished on the wains.

Father laughing, mother crying.

Mother screaming. Mother silent.

Coats over heads.

It's okay Claire don't be scared.

It's okay Alan don't be scared.

Strong arms around him. Safe now.

Don't be scared wee man, I'm here now. You're safe now.

Brown eye smiling. Green eye smiling.

Mother screaming, father shouting.

Alan crying. Alan dying.

Chapter 7

Friday 12 March 1965

Scooter Boy was Purple Heart Drunk – A Leeds teenager whose motor scooter collided with a car admitted to police that he had taken 'purple heart' tablets earlier in the evening, Leeds magistrates were told. Police were called to the incident in Stanningley after the driver of the car, Mr. Barry Eastman suspected that 18 year old Colin Hartshead was intoxicated. Hartshead denied drinking but admitted to taking the tablets at a coffee bar earlier in the evening and was fined £20 for careless driving by magistrate Mr.A.E.Knowles

The double-knock on Keith Connolly's flat door fractured the awkward silence which had descended after Alan had replayed the scene in Morrison's hardware store to his brother, and promised Wesley, Norman and Scotty that he'd be making some changes to the operation.

"That'll be the drop-off now." Keith Connolly stood and left the room and the sound of muffled conversation increased in volume until he returned, followed by a middle aged man wearing a black leather trenchcoat and carrying a brown holdall. Tall, early fifties, with hair too dark for his age and brylcreamed into a neat quiff, he sniffed the air like a predator detecting the fear of concealed prey. Alan's eyes widened as the man removed a red cravat to reveal the black and white of a clerical collar.

"Father Ernest." Wesley, Normal and Scotty averted their eyes and muttered a greeting from the settee. The man ignored them and turned towards Alan.

"You're the brother then."

"Keith's brother, yes."

"What denomination are you?"

"Erm, denomination...what, erm..?" Alan was unnerved by the man's unwavering stare and the impact his arrival had on the other lads.

"Do you go to church?" The man cut across his stammered response.

"I...erm, I used to, I..."

"You're a Catholic like him?" The man nodded towards Keith who was lurking in the doorway.

"Well, erm, aye, I was...I am."

"Good. Go to church. Save yourself." The man's voice was reduced to a barely audible whisper as he bent towards Alan and placed a hand gently upon his head. He then turned and handed the holdall to Keith and left without uttering another word.

The room remained silent until a thud and click from the hallway indicated that the outside door had been closed.

"Has he definitely gone?" Wesley inquired and Keith peered nervously around the door frame.

"Yeah he's gone." Keith unzipped the bag and removed a polythene bag filled with blue capsules.

"Who the fuck was that?" Alan was smiling but the faces of the others remained deadly serious.

"Fucking Father Ernest. Jesus, what's he doing making the drop?" Scotty stood up and pulled back the net curtains to furtively peer down into the Quarry Hill flats car park. "Reckon Donovan sent him to check out Alan?"

"Fuck knows, but I don't want him in my flat, I'm going to have to get it exorcised by a proper priest!" Keith attempted unsuccessfully to lift the mood.

"So who is he?"

Keith retrieved two more polythene bags from the holdall and placed them on the coffee table. "Father Ernest is Clive Donovan's right-hand man. Mr.Donovan is very keen on his religion, thinks it's important to stay in the big man's good books for when the final reckoning comes. Ernest is like his own personal parish priest."

"A drug dealing priest?" Alan looked confused.

"He's no fucking priest. Rumour is he did a couple of months in a seminary at 'start of 'war to avoid getting called up. Then he left and became a conscientious objector, that's how he met Donovan. They both used their supposed religious beliefs to avoid 'call up." Scotty turned back from the window.

"That's where Mr.Donovan made his money. All the main players in the Leeds underworld joined up, Donovan and Father Ernest stayed here and cleaned up in the black market, selling stuff to the yanks. It was the perfect cover story, no one expected a couple of peace-loving Christians to be major gangsters." Keith shook his head in admiration as he tore open one of the polythene bags and scooped out a handful of pills.

"And their links with 'yanks meant they were able to build up a right arsenal of weapons, so when 'war ended and 'others started coming home, they were well prepared for a war on 'streets." Norman tossed a blue pill into the air, caught it in his mouth and swallowed.

"Wiped out all their competition by the start of '47 by all accounts." Keith reached across the coffee table and removed the bag of pills from Norman's grasp.

"Right time, right place, right idea. Perfect." Alan leant back on the couch with his hands behind his head, lost in admiration of the wartime sleight of hand which had created a criminal empire. *Ideas and Bravery. Success. Fucking genius.*

"So now you know brother. Make sure you tell Father Ernest you've been going to church regularly. You don't want to get on the wrong side of him, believe me." Keith grimaced. "Right then, time for work..."

"What's the plan then?" Alan reached across and picked up one of the polythene bags from the table.

Keith extended his right hand to invite Scotty to lead the briefing and retreated to lean on the window-sill.

"Right then..." Scotty stood and picked up one of the bags. "There's been no Purple Hearts around since Autumn and all 'scare stories in 'papers. French Blues make up most of our business now. It's basically 'same stuff as 'Hearts', Drynamil it's called, but 'pills are light blue now with a line down 'middle. We knock them out at 1/6." Scotty picked a tablet out of the bag and held it up to the light then tossed it to Alan, who popped it in his mouth.

Scotty reached down to the table and picked up another bag to retrieve a yellow capsule."Dexes are as good as blues but they aren't as popular, so we only sell them for

1/." He tossed the capsule to Alan, who struggled to swallow it and coughed as he got off the couch and headed into the kitchen, where he filled a tea cup with water. He was followed by Scotty who held a black capsule between his forefinger and thumb.

"Black Bomber. The champagne of 'uppers. We were getting some called black and greens before Christmas but these all-black ones are 'best. They go for 2/ but a lot of kids won't take them. Most lasses don't want them, think they'll get addicted or summat!" Scotty popped the pill in his mouth and took the cup of water from Alan.

"We don't just cater for the night time market either, we also look after our customers' Sunday and Monday morning requirements." Keith reached into the holdall and withdrew a polythene bag filled with bright red capsules. "Seconal. Kids call them reds for obvious reasons. You need a few of these to take the edge off after a long weekend. We sometimes get other types, Mogadon or Mandrax, but these are the most common."

"How many are we shifting a night then?" Alan directed the question to his brother and the lads all looked towards Keith, lighting a cigarette while leaning on the window sill.

"Well, there's over a thousand pills in those bags, and I'll be disappointed if we aren't asking Mr.Donovan for some more by Sunday morning."

Alan did some mental arithmetic and whistled in appreciation.

"Aye brother, there's some serious money to be made. It's a good earner."

"Good for some." Norman muttered under his breath.

"If you don't like it pal, you know what you can do." Keith exhaled a cloud of smoke as Norman scowled and looked at his feet.

 "Go have a word with the priest and Mr.Donovan and see how that ends for you eh? For fucks sake man, you spend your time in places you'd be going to anyway, get your pills for free and you get paid for it. Doesn't sound bad to me. What do you think brother?"

Alan looked from his brother to Norman who was still staring at the floor.

"I think there's probably some improvements can be made to the operation that will benefit everyone. I'm looking forward to hitting the town and seeing how it all works."

Keith Connolly nodded and smiled. "That's why I asked you to come down here. I knew you'd shake things up a bit."

Alan stood up, picked up his parka and pointed the rest of the lads towards the door.

"Oh I'll certainly do that brother, just you watch me."

Chapter 8

Saturday, 13 March 1965

Price Spiral Steadied-It is clear that the pace of the prices spiral of the past few months has been stopped, said Economic Secretary George Brown today. The index of retail prices from February indicated that the Prices and Income Review Board have steadied the spiral and brought it to some extent under control. "Wages and salaries were trying to keep pace with the prices, and each was following the other. We hope to have broken that cycle," said Mr. Brown.

"Three games in six days is mad. I tell you, 'fucking FA are determined to make sure Leeds win nowt this season." Wesley spat and flicked his cigarette into the road as he, Norman and Alan walked past Jacomelli's Aloha Bar on Boar Lane.

"Good timing getting Peacock back though. Another goal today and two in 'cup game in midweek." Norman paused to tap the window to attract the attention of the bedraggled parrot tethered to a perch in the doorway.

"Yeah but looks like Bremner, Charlton and Storrie might all be out for Burnley on Monday. It's a conspiracy, I tell you."

"Still top of the league though?" Alan had studied the table in the Evening Post and was keen to show that he was keeping track of Leeds' unexpected success in their first season back in the top flight.

"Yeah, but Chelsea and Man U have both played a game less and they have much better goal average than us.

We'll need to win it outright on points I reckon." Wesley pushed open the door of the Del Rio and the three youths began to unzip their parkas as they descended the steps.

"Fucking hell Scotty, what happened?"

Scotty forced a rueful half smile through a swollen lip and grimaced as Chantelle, the French student waitress, dabbed at a cut above his eye with a damp cloth.

"Cohen and his mates is what happened."

"Bastard! When was this? They've made a right mess of your shirt..." Norman pointed out a red rosette of blood on Scotty's white collar.

"Half an hour ago. I parked 'scooter over 'street and was just about to come in when they all piled out of 'door."

"So who is this Cohen?" Alan's right hand subconsciously reached into the lining of his parka, feeling the reassuring weight of the bayonet. *Switch flicked, electrical charge crackling into life. Voices starting to whisper.*

"He's the lad whose scooter your riding, and he isn't happy about it. Especially that I took all his shit off it. The flyscreen had his and his bird's name on it, he was properly pissed off that I slung that."

"Where is he now?" Alan Connolly took a deep breath. *Use your head. Don't get nicked for anything stupid.*

"They'll be back up at Cro-Magnon coffee bar at Moortown corner. That's where they hang out. They don't come in town much."

"Right, well they won't come in town again when we've finished with them, but that can wait for another day. We've got work to do tonight." Alan nodded towards the door and Scotty groaned as he hauled himself from the wooden seat, before turning to the large figure in the sheepskin coat who was lighting up the pinball table.

"Cheers mate. I owe you one." He patted the young man on the shoulder but received no response.

"He saved my life. They dragged me down 'steps and were kicking 'shit out of me. Chantelle tried to stop them but they just knocked her over. Next thing, 'pinball had stopped pinging and he appeared out of nowhere, smacked a couple of them and picked Cohen up and threw him over a table. Then chased them all out of 'door."

"What's your name big man?" Alan raised his voice above the sound of bells and buzzers but the tall, heavyset figure remained unresponsive.

"We don't know his name. He comes in every day and plays the pinball non-stop. He never speaks." Chantelle lowered her voice and dabbed at a smear of blood on Scotty's eyebrow as he picked up his parka.

Alan took a step towards the pinball machine "I like a man who can look after himself but doesn't shout about it. I could probably put some work your way if you're interested pal. Let me know..."

He turned and followed the others towards the door, only to pause as the pinball fell silent.

"Nigel. My name's Nigel." The young man spoke softly as he momentarily turned from the machine to face Alan.

"Nice to meet you, Nigel. Non-Stop Nigel, that's a good name...see us in here tomorrow at midday. I've got a wee job for you to help us out with."

Chapter 9

The explosive opening chords of 'Can't Explain' seemed to punch a hole in the Three Coins speakers and propelled the entire black-walled bar into a jerking, sweat-soaked frenzy.

Alan Connolly shoved another stick of chewing gum into his mouth, teeth grinding in time to the music as Daltrey's vocals kicked in. Cool, confident, aggressive, totally in control. Only a mod could write a song like that. He'd graduated from French Blues to Bombers at around midnight and now, three hours later, he was struggling to remember whether he'd had three or four of them.

His shirt stuck to his back and condensation dripped from the low ceiling and into his coke glass as he watched Scotty holding court with a gang of lads in the corner next to the stage, and Norman's increasingly erratic dancing caused some disapproving glances has he waved his arms and crashed into dancing couples.

"Good night mate?" Wesley appeared beside him holding a bottle of water.

"What d' you say?" Alan struggled to hear above the feedback as Townsend's guitar made the speakers buzz louder than the feedback in his head.

"I said it's been a good night. Shifted loads of pills, The Dawnbreakers were good earlier, and this lad is playing some great tunes."

"Aye, I think I'm going to like it down here." Alan allowed himself a smile.

"Well, it might be about to get even better..." Wesley beckoned to a girl stood outside the ladies toilet and she pushed her way through the crowd to join them. She was small and plump, with heavily mascaraed eyes beneath a short, straight blonde fringe. She wore clumpy 'granny' shoes and carried a square, box-like vanity case.

"This is Elaine. She works in 'office for Leeds United."

"Ah yeah, this is your bird that Keith told us about. Alright love?" Alan shouted the question to no one and avoided eye contact with the girl, directing his words towards Wesley's right ear. He'd had a girlfriend, Jenny, but that was at school, and she'd not kept in touch when he was sent to borstal. He'd not been on a date for over three years and wasn't really sure how to speak to girls or what to talk about.

"She's not really my bird. She sorts us out with tickets for 'big matches when we need them and gets me a programme every week. You need them for 'tokens. Good customer too...she's quite partial to a few blues on a weekend." Wesley leant in and cupped his hand around Alan's ear to ensure his words were heard above the music. "Anyway, she's got a mate, Chrissy, she fancies you."

Alan felt a knot of apprehension tighten in his stomach.

"Oh aye, what's she like then?" Alan scanned the dancefloor and rubbed at his jaw which was starting to ache from six hours of non-stop gum chewing.

"She's powdering her nose. Be back in a minute." Wesley nodded towards the ladies toilet and winked at Alan, then took hold of Elaine's hand and leant in, cupping his hand around her ear as he spoke, causing her to giggle.

The mood shifted as the rasping voice of James Brown burst out of the speakers, inviting the dancers aboard the Night Train, and Alan felt the apprehension building inside him as he stared at the flashing lights, *Red, Green, Purple*, the train-horn blast of the saxophone setting his heart racing. *Calm down, Calm down. It's just a girl.*

"I've had enough for tonight mate, I think I'll be away to my bed." He didn't wait for a response from Wesley and began to push his way through the crowd, the knot in his stomach tightening, heart thumping louder than the music.

"Watch where you're going you clumsy sod!" Alan turned to see a youth, pencil-thin in his fat uncle's cheap suit, brushing a spilled drink from his sleeve. His girlfriend, a hard faced girl in dark framed glasses, shook her head and mouthed incomprehensible, angry words. Alan felt the first wave of electricity overcoming the nervousness in the pit of his stomach. *Power switch flicked, voices too loud to ignore. Fucking straights, fuck them.*

"You fucking what?" He turned to face the young man and the crowd around them began to part in anticipation of what would inevitably follow.

"You spilt my drink, pushing past like that." The youth took a step backwards and turned the sleeve of his jacket towards Alan to display a large damp stain.

"Spilt your fucking drink eh? Do you know who I am son?" Alan picked up an empty coke bottle and smashed it on a table, then brandished the jagged neck as he advanced towards the couple, their faces illuminated in the flashing lights. *Red, Green, Purple. Electricity surging, current coursing through his veins, white light blinding. No Prisoners.*

Someone screamed behind him, and the music seemed to increase in volume, train-horn sax screaming, as the boy raised his hands and began to retreat, leaving his girlfriend frozen in Alan's path. His first reaction to the arm around his neck was to swing the broken bottle at the figure who was restraining him, but the first word he heard halted his advance.

"Boss! Boss, leave it."

Alan turned to see Wesley's face inches from his own.

"Leave it Alan, it's not worth getting kicked out for."

Behind Wesley stood Elaine, eyes wide and hands over her mouth, and another girl, small and pretty with dark hair cut short and tousled in an urchin cut.

"The bouncer's coming, get on 'dance floor." Wesley shoved Alan forward and followed by the two girls they threaded their way through the mass of bodies as Betty Everett's 'Getting Mighty Crowded' replaced James Brown to slow the tempo.

"Quick, dance with Chrissie." Wesley shoved Alan towards the girl who looked up at him with fearful eyes as Wesley steered Elaine away to the other side of the dancefloor.

"Sorry." Alan leant forward and shouted into Christine's ear, catching the scent of old perfume mingled with hair lacquer and sweat. She smiled and shook her head, mouthing words he couldn't hear, but he knew she understood, and he looked into her eyes and immediately felt the connection.

"Want a pill?" It was all he could think to say, but she shook her head and he wondered if he'd messed it up again, but as the pace picked up with the Kingsmen and 'Louie Louie,' he caught her exchanging a knowing smile with Elaine before she took his hand and pulled him in close.

It seemed like they'd only been dancing for minutes when the lights flashed and Alan checked his watch.

"Quarter to five. I need to go." Chrissie's breath tickled his neck as she pulled him down lower to shout in his ear. Before he could respond, she kissed him on the cheek and followed Elaine towards the cloakroom without looking back.

"Told you, you're in there pal." Wesley appeared beside him.

"Aye, she's nice, I think. I've not really said much to her though."

"Well, I'm giving Elaine a ride home so she's going to be on her own. I'd get in there before someone else does."

Wesley had barely finished speaking before Alan nodded and squeezed his arm.

"See you at the Del Rio at twelve tomorrow, we'll sort this Cohen thing out." He shouted over his shoulder and headed through the sweating dancefloor crowd.

The early March chill froze the sweat on his body as he turned right, then left and jogged down Basinghall Street towards the Del Rio where his scooter was parked. Turning left onto Boar Lane, he spotted Christine trying to flag a cab at the top of Mill Hill.

"You need a ride?"

"You're Scotch." She giggled, hearing his accent clearly for the first time.

"Aye, Glasgow...so you need a ride home then?"

"It's too cold, I can get a cab." She flicked at her short fringe and he was able to see her face under the glow of the orange street lamp, ghostly white, stripped of make-up apart from dark mascara beneath eyebrows plucked into thin arched lines.

Her half smile said he needed to try harder so he turned off the ignition.

"You'll have to think of another excuse." Alan slowly and deliberately swung his leg from the scooter, clicked the key backwards in the lock and flicked open the seat to retrieve the parka which he held out towards the shivering girl.

"As long as you drive slow, it's icy." Christine stepped forward, then pulled on the parka and climbed onto the back of the scooter.

Alan smiled as they headed over Leeds Bridge and he felt her hand on his waist. Whipped raw by an icy wind, he felt himself shaking and didn't know if it was the cold or the pills or both but he didn't care.

A new start. New town, new job, new scooter, new girl. Wesley calling him 'boss'. The music still playing in his head. *Got a feeling inside. I can't explain.*

Chapter 10

Sunday 14 March 1965

The blast of a klaxon horn over his right shoulder caused Alan Connolly to squeeze the brake of the Lambretta as the four scooters climbed Harrogate Road's slight incline on the approach to Moortown Corner.

Pulling alongside him, Wesley nodded left towards a building with a pointed gable on the corner of a parade of shops. A row of six parked scooters identified the Cro-Magnon coffee bar, and Alan flicked on the indicator and turned left at the traffic lights, pulling up round the corner from the café.

He rolled the scooter into a space and hauled it onto its centre stand, then watched as Wesley pulled in beside him, closely followed by Scotty, with Norman bringing up the rear, his Vespa struggling under the additional weight of Non-Stop Nigel riding pillion.

"Enjoy that Nigel?" Alan grinned as the big man silently dismounted, flattening a thick shock of dark hair with a huge, gloved hand.

"Right lads, turn the scooters round. We might need to make a quick getaway."

"Shit Alan, we don't know how many of them there are in there. I'll never get away with Nigel on the back." Norman's eyes darted nervously towards the café.

"Don't worry about that, Cohen and his lads won't be following us when we've done with them, but the owners might ring the law." Alan popped the seat of the Lambretta and removed a hammer, a truncheon and a thick chain with attached padlock. "Choose your tools boys."

"Fuck, I'm not sure about this..." Wesley stopped mid-sentence as he caught Alan's eye, and Non-Stop Nigel extended his hand and took hold of the truncheon.

"That's the spirit big man." Alan smiled and passed the hammer to Wesley then held the chain out towards Scotty who was tucking his parka hood into the back of the coat.

"So they can't pull it over your head while you're scrapping." Wesley and Norman nodded and followed suit.

"Come on lads. Let's teach these cunts a lesson." Alan set off towards the corner without looking behind him. *Power on, current buzzing, the voices too loud to ignore. No prisoners. No fucking prisoners.*

Their arrival at the Cro-Magnon coffee bar was announced by a wooden signboard advertising hot and cold refreshments and fresh sandwiches exploding into the café amidst a shower of shattered glass from the front window.

Youths in parkas and striped blazers and girls in white stockings and knee length skirts screamed in terror as they sprang from their seats, their arms covering their heads. A young man in a pork-pie hat instinctively tossed a tray of hot drinks in the direction of the five figures who kicked open the door and charged forward, brandishing an assortment of weapons. The tray bounced off the sleeve of Nigel's sheepskin coat and he made a beeline for the young man in the hat, bringing the truncheon down hard on the crown of his head.

"Cohen! Which one of you is Cohen?" Alan stood at the front of the group, bayonet extended, scanning the faces of the dozen youths who were cowering in front of the counter. A man in his thirties and of middle eastern appearance shuffled sideways and reached for the telephone.

"I'd put that down my friend if you want to keep both your hands." Alan stepped forward and the man slowly replaced the receiver.

"So, Cohen, show yourself..." Alan held the bayonet forward, his arm extended, waving it menacingly in the faces of the cowering Moortown mods, who remained silent.

"Cohen...I'm guessing you're a Jew boy?" Alan scanned the wide-eyed faces before him and his wild stare settled on a tall youth with an olive complexion and dark rings beneath his eyes. "Is it you lad? Are you Cohen?"

Alan stepped forward and the young man's face crumpled and he began to cry.

"It's me." A voice from the left caused Alan to pause.

"I'm Martin Cohen." Alan turned to face the boy who stepped forward from the group. Late teens, wearing white sta-prest slacks and a red Fred Perry polo short under a blue cardigan with a yellow 'Y' on the chest, he'd attempted to tame the slight wave in his hair with lacquer, which suspended a heavy fringe just above his narrow eyes.

"And you're the kid who's riding my scooter." Cohen's voice sounded confident, but his bottom lip quivered slightly, betraying his fear.

"I'm not a kid...I'm Alan Connolly, and it's not your scooter anymore, it's mine. Because you couldn't afford to pay for it, could you? Think you're a face but you're just a third-class ticket, son. Too many lamps and mirrors, and a fucking fly-screen. Do you think it's still 63?" Connolly smirked and licked his lips as he stepped forward, the bayonet extended before him and the Moortown mods stepped aside, leaving Connolly facing Cohen, whose hands trembled visibly.

"Scotty did you a favour clearing all that shite off it. It looks alright now. A proper scooter for a real face, a high number. And there's you, thinking you can come into town and lay your hands on one of my boys, and get away with it..." Connolly raised his eyebrows indicating that he expected an answer, but Cohen remained silent, blinking quickly, clenching his fists in anticipation of the violence he knew was sure to follow.

"Is that what you think Martin? That you and your lads can batter Scotty and escape any sort of retribution? Because if that's what you think..." Alan shook his head and stepped forward, his mouth curled into a snarl.

"If that's what you think, you're about to learn a very painful lesson." Cohen extended his hands in a futile attempt to protect his face as Alan slowly raised the bayonet. A girl's scream provided the soundtrack to Alan's assault as he swung the blade, Cohen ducking and deflecting the blow with his forearm, before finding his escape route blocked by a table, still containing steaming mugs and sauce bottles. He turned to find Connolly advancing, swinging the bayonet in wide arcs, the excited faces of his gang behind, urging him on. In a blind, adrenaline fuelled panic, Martin Cohen hit the table at speed and found himself tumbling forward, hot coffee scalding his face, hitting the floor, a stabbing pain along his arm as his wrist bent under him.

"No!" Martin Cohen twisted on the wet tiled floor and looked upwards into the dark eyes of his attacker, his white sta-prest now stained by his own piss, as a wide smile appeared on Alan Connolly's face. Connolly raised the bayonet and Cohen closed his eyes and began to cry.

"Stop! You boy...I'm talking to you."

The voice was one of authority, a command not a request. Alan heard Scotty say 'oh shit' close behind him, and turned as Father Ernest stepped forward, crunching broken glass and crockery into the lino.

"Give me that." He held out his hand and Alan paused, looking from the point of the bayonet to the man in the clerical collar and black leather trench coat, then to Cohen, laying back on the floor, tears on his cheeks, a yellow stain spreading on his white trousers.

"I said give me that." Father Ernest's raised voice and black, shark eyes told Alan that he had little choice. He held the bayonet upright and extended his arm, allowing the fake priest to take hold of the handle.

"Come with me." Father Ernest turned, his black patent leather shoes crunching glass, and Alan followed him out of the door.

Chapter 11

"Get in." Father Ernest held open the rear door of the black Rover P5 parked outside the Cro-Magnon coffee bar. A couple in a Ford Anglia waiting at the Moortown Corner lights stared at the priest brandishing the Japanese bayonet then turned away quickly.

"I'll go sort out this mess with Kostas," Ernest stooped and spoke softly into the car, then stepped back to allow Alan to climb into the back seat, where he was immediately met by a cloud of exhaled cigarette smoke.

Alan blinked and assessed his fellow passenger. Late fifties or early sixties, with thick, wavy white hair, worn too long for his age and slicked back with Brylcream. A thin, pale face with small round eyes, made almost cartoon-like by bulbous pink lips, cracked and dry. The man remained silent as he exhaled smoke through his nose and breathed noisily before turning to look at Alan.

"Clive Donovan." When he eventually spoke, the words were almost inaudible, his mouth opening slightly to reveal brown-stained teeth concealed behind a curtain of stringy saliva strands which stuck to his inflated lips.

"Pleased to meet you Mr Donovan, I'm..." Alan's introduction was curtailed by Clive Donovan's raised hand.

"I know who you are. You're the brother." He took another drag on his cigarette, then muttered something so softly that Alan wasn't even sure he'd spoken.

"Yes I'm..."

"Employees fighting." Donovan raised his voice slightly and two tendrils of smoke drifted from his nostrils.

Alan was still thinking of how to respond as Donovan continued, his voice again almost too soft to hear.

"Two of my employees fighting, like rats in a sack. Unacceptable." Donovan tilted his head to watch the Moortown mods and their girls emerge from the coffee bar and stand in a chattering semi-circle in front of the broken window.

"I didn't know he worked for you..."

Donovan's gazed remained on the café and he nodded slowly.

"Young Martin heads up my operation in North Leeds. Does the same job as you'll be doing in town. Was it about his motorbike?"

"Motorbike?"

"You're riding his motorbike are you not?"

"It's a scooter."

"Scooter, motorbike. Same thing..."

"It's a Lambretta, a motorbike is..." Again, Alan's explanation ended abruptly as Donovan raised his hand.

"I don't care." Donovan slowly wound down the window to flick out his cigarette and the silence in the car was broken by the gentle chatter of the crowd on the pavement.

"You've been to prison." Donovan turned to face Alan for the first time and he felt his face redden.

"Aye, how did you know?"

"You stink of it." Donovan retrieved a cigarette from a silver case and held it between his index and middle finger, closing his eyes as he inhaled and the tip glowed orange.

"Stink of it. It's all about you. A stench of depravity." He regarded Alan with disgust.

"I don't like the smell of prison Alan. And I don't like my employees fighting in the streets. It's bad for business. Do you understand?"

Alan tried to speak but his mouth was so dry that no words came. He nodded, but Donovan was looking ahead again as Father Ernest emerged from the coffee bar in conversation with Martin Cohen.

"Your brother assured me you could do a job for me. All I've seen so far is trouble. And I don't need trouble Alan. Do you see?" Donovan's hand rested on Alan's knee causing the hairs on the back of his neck to prickle.

"I'm sorry Mr. Donovan. I've got a few ideas. Things we can improve in town..." Alan swallowed hard as Clive Donovan tightened his grip, gently squeezing his knee.

"Good boy...that's what we like to hear." Donovan turned again and his bulbous lips retracted to display crooked rows of tar-stained teeth, too close now and Alan felt himself recoil.

The car fell silent again, but Donovan's hand remained on Alan's leg, as Father Ernest ruffled Cohen's lacquered hair and walked back towards the car.

He opened the door and got into the driver's seat without turning round.

"Reverend, our young friend is in need of guidance."
Donovan leant forward and whispered, his hand now
removed from Alan's knee. Father Ernest swivelled
awkwardly in the driver's seat, his coat squeaking on the
fake leather. He held out his right hand, a bluebird tattoo
visible between thumb and index finger.

"Take his hand." Clive Donovan whispered in Alan's ear
and he smelt sweat and old smoke, and slowly raised his
own right hand, forcing himself not to pull it away as
Father Ernest gripped it, his palm cold and damp.

"Close your eyes." Donovan's hand back on his knee.
Alan struggled to control his breathing as he dipped his
head, eyes shut tight, Father Ernest's voice deep and low.

*'Lord, we pray for our brother, Alan, for he walks in sin
today.*

*Help him understand that his sin serves to diminish the
voice of your son, our saviour.*

*Help him to crave your presence more than he craves
sin.'*

"The stench of sin and depravity, all about you."
Donovan's breath on his cheek, his voice soft in his ear.

*'Help him grow in the fruit of the Spirit and walk closer
with Yourself, heavenly father.*

Show him his vanity and grant him humility.

'Show him the light, bring him in from the darkness.

"This darkness all about you." Donovan gently touching
his hair.

*'Help him to renounce Satan and all his work and
ways.*

57

Guide his path Lord, for he is our child. '

"You're our child." Donovan's lips gently touching his ear, the words whispered in his ear.

'For the love of thine only son, our saviour, Jesus Christ. Amen.'

Alan could still feel Donovan's fetid breath on his cheek and didn't dare open his eyes until Father Ernest released the grip on his hand. Eyes opened, he stared ahead at Scotty, Wesley and Norman who stood aside from the crowd, casting concerned glances towards the car. Non-stop Nigel had positioned himself, arms folded, between the two groups and the Moortown mods glanced warily in his direction.

"Go now." Donovan hissed in his ear and Alan gratefully reached for the door handle.

"And remember, no trouble. Bad for business."

Alan clambered unsteadily from the back seat and slammed the car door shut, then paused and tapped on the driver's window.

"Mr Donovan...can I have my bayonet back please?"

Chapter 12

Dark. Awake. Three now not two.

The monster is here.

Claire crying.

Beer and whiskey, smoke and sweat.

Hands on his neck. Hands on his waist.

Coats over his head.

Don't be scared wee man.

Claire crying. Father breathing.

Ya dirty bastard.

Strong arms around him. Not safe now.
Never safe again.

Chapter 13

Monday 15 March 1965

*Two Leeds clubs at Wembley Would be Great for City
says Lord Mayor - Leeds United and Hunslet for the FA
And RL Challenge cups! This unprecedented sporting
prospect was today heralded by Mrs L.Naylor, Lord
Mayor of the city, which now has representatives in the
semi-finals of the two competitions. The Lord Mayor,
who saw Hunslet's victory over Leeds at Parkside on
Saturday, and who will be making her second visit of
the season to Elland Road tonight for United's
important league clash with Burnley has followed the
fortunes of both teams for a number of years.*

Alan Connolly stared down the silver barrel of the pistol
pointing directly at his face from the back seat of the
Ford Zodiac. He raised his hands and smiled at the dark-
haired boy in the cowboy hat.

"You're not going to shoot me are you sheriff?"

The child closed one eye and carefully took aim before
pulling the trigger three times, causing a red reel of caps
to revolve in the barrel.

"You love the cowboys don't you Maxie? Can't get him
away from the TV when Gunsmoke is on can we?" Terry
Jackson took aim at his son with two fingers and
returned fire.

"You got the stuff then?"

"In the boot." Jackson fingered a set of keys and walked to the rear of the Zodiac, the boot opened with a clunk, and both men peered in.

"This is standard 12 ounce worsted. I could have got 9 ounce but that would be no good for winter on that thing." Terry nodded across the car park towards the Lambretta parked in the shadow of Quarry Hill flats, and Alan reached into the boot and rubbed the material between thumb and forefinger.

"Feels good quality, right enough."

"The best. Straight out of 'door of 'mill in Shipley. I told you, 'wife's brother is 'foreman, you won't get wool of this standard for a better price."

"And there's enough there for suits for all the lads?"

"Yep, even enough for that big fella you've got working with you. How do the others feel about taking a pay cut to give him a share?" Terry Jackson folded his arms and rested his backside on the car boot.

"They haven't worked it out yet, but I'm hoping they won't have to."

"How's that then?"

Alan smiled. "The big guy and the suits is all part of my new strategy for the team. No one respects those scruffy wee cunts at the moment. Step one is to smarten them up. Step two is providing a more visible warning of what happens to businesses that don't pay."

Terry Jackson nodded his approval. "Makes sense, but your percentage stays the same, so you've still got more mouths to feed. And that big kid will take some feeding..."

"And step 3 is to increase our income. We clamp down hard on missed payments, if you miss a week, your premium goes up. If you still don't pay, penalties will be harsh and highly visible to act as an example to others. And I'm going to change how we shift the pills. No more strolling round town mob handed. I'm giving each of them their own patch. That helps me see who's pulling their weight and also which places we're selling more at. We can put the prices up in them."

"You've got it all worked out."

Terry Jackson retrieved a brown paper parcel from the car boot and tore it open....and you asked for something a bit special for yourself? This is a 33% kid mohair mix. Two tone, you see?" He held the fabric to the light and tilted it. "No one else will have that exact same shade, I promise you."

Alan smiled. That was what it was all about. He was a stylist, an innovator. Not some plastic mod who bought their suits off the peg at John Collier or Harry Fenton's.

"Anyway, who are you going to get to make them up for you?" Jackson scooped up the suit lengths in both arms and handed them to Alan.

"Not sure yet but we've got a few tailors on the books haven't we?"

"Three or four in town I think."

"Good. I'm going to make one of them a proposition he can't refuse. I'll get the cash to you by the end of the week." *You'll be working for me within two years, Terry Jackson. Tick Tock.*

Chapter 14

Arthur Littlewood's eyes seemed too wide for his thin face, on account of the thick lenses of his horn-rimmed spectacles. Now, in his tailor's shop in Kirkgate, he stared unblinking at the group of young men who stood before him.

"So let me get this right." A hand rolled cigarette balanced precariously in the corner of his mouth as he spoke. "You want me to make you each a suit, using that cloth, and not charge you for any of them?"

"Correct." Alan Connolly rested a hand on the suit lengths he'd placed on the bench and smiled.

"And why on earth would you think I'd even consider doing that?" Arthur removed the cigarette from his lips and watched a thin wisp of smoke rise from the tip in a shaft of light edging through the curtains.

"It's a great opportunity, and the boys tell me you're the main man to go to for made-to-measure suits around here, so I've decided to reward you with the contract."

Arthur Littlewood laughed quietly to himself and walked to the door, which opened with a clanking bell. He held it ajar.

"Well, thanks for the offer boys, but the answer is no thanks."

Alan caught Nigel's eye and Arthur stepped back as the large figure in the sheepskin coat leant across him and shoved the door closed.

"Alright, so obviously I haven't fully explained the opportunity I'm presenting you with." Alan pulled up a chair and sat down.

"How many tailors are in Leeds City centre?"

"No idea." Arthur took another roll-up from a tin and lit it, the tip glowing orange in the lens of his glasses.

"Well, if you include all the shops that make suits, I'd say there are about twenty. And more than half of those are our clients, as are you."

Arthur grunted and wobbled his head.

"What if all the mods in Leeds only used one tailor?" Alan stood up and picked up a large pair of scissors.

"He'd be quite busy, I suppose." Arthur blinked quickly behind the thick lenses, his eyes focused on the moving blades of the scissors.

"Very busy. And he could charge a bit more, maybe a lot more." Alan clicked the scissors in front of Arthur's nose.

"But why would these mods only use one tailor?"

"Because the rest would all refuse their business. Those tailors would be told in no uncertain terms that if they were heard to be making a suit for anyone in a parka.. anyone riding a scooter... " Alan looked to his friends for a contribution.

"Anyone in a waisted jacket, Levi's and desert boots..." Wesley chipped in.

"Maybe any lad wearing a Ben Sherman or Fred Perry shirt..." Scotty rubbed his chin and Alan nodded.

"Basically, any tailor making a suit for someone who looks in any way like a mod, would have to bear the consequences, which at best, could be an increase in what they pay us. And at worst..." Alan slowly lifted the scissors above his right shoulder and snipped at a pair of trousers hanging on a rail above him.

"Oh bloody hell, no!" Arthur Littlewood's cigarette fell from his mouth as he looked down at the severed trouser leg lying on the floorboards.

"So, basically one tailor would get all the business from every mod in Leeds. And he wouldn't have his rent increased...or risk an unfortunate accident occurring on his premises."

"Oh Jesus...and this would be a one-off? I make these suits and that's it?" Arthur trod on the cigarette end and stooped to pick up the trouser leg.

"For the lads, yes that will do for now. For me, I'll probably be needing one a month."

Arthur Littlewood sighed and reached for his tape measure.

"It doesn't seem like I've got much choice does it?"

Alan Connolly stood up and extended his hand.

"Congratulations Arthur, you made the right choice. I look forward to a long and fruitful relationship between us. Now get sewing."

Chapter 15

Tuesday 16 March 1965

US Planes Blast North Vietnam Targets Again- Saigon, Monday- US Aircraft today raided military installations in North Vietnam for the second successive day. Officials said the raid was in retaliation for acts of sabotage and terrorism by the communists in South Vietnam. A US spokesman declined to say which targets were hit, how many planes took part, or whether all the aircraft returned safely.

"Looking good in those suits boys!" Alan Connolly's arrival caused Wesley, Norman and Scotty to momentarily divert their attention from the girls on the Arcade Mecca dancefloor, as he and Non-stop Nigel joined them on the balcony. "No one is going to respect you if you look like a bunch of scruffy wee cunts. Worse than that though, you won't respect yourselves. You look the part now." Alan straightened the lapels on Norman's suit jacket, then tightened his tie.

"I can't believe how busy it is on a lunchtime." Alan leant over to survey the scene as the DJ replaced 'Concrete and Clay' by Unit 4+2 with 'Downtown,' the sound of Petula Clark's voice driving the few male dancers from the floor.

"The music's shit, too much chart stuff, but you get plenty of lasses in on their lunchbreak." Norman was clutching a Vallance's bag.

"Just bought the Marvelettes new EP. You heard it?"

"Yeah, Radio Caroline played a couple of songs off it last night." Alan ran his finger down his parting and smoothed down his fringe as he watched an older man in a white suit, his collar length hair dyed in black and white checks, chatting to two teenage girls wearing the blue pinafore uniforms of Lewis's cosmetics counter. "Are they here yet Wes?"

"Yeah, there's only three of them though. They're down in the El Rio having a coffee." Wesley led the way with a nod of his head.

"I told you they'd be here, that Greenhoff kid fancies Elaine. He'll follow her anywhere."

Entering through an archway, Alan spotted Elaine sat at a low table with three young men. Definitely not mods, they had the clean-cut appearance of junior office managers or Peace Corps volunteers.

A playful hair tug from Wesley caused Elaine to squeal and turn around and he planted a big kiss on her lips, while staring at the fresh-faced blond boy sat next to her.

"Drinks anyone?" Alan produced a wallet from his jacket pocket.

"I'll have another coke float please Alan." Elaine handed him an empty glass which was immediately passed to Nigel.

"Here Norman, take Nigel and get everyone a drink." Alan handed over a pound note and Norman addressed the group.

"Drinks lads?"

The young men shook their heads and from their muttered collective thanks-but-no-thanks, Alan detected a Scottish accent.

"Where are you from then pal?" He addressed a youth in his mid-teens with a side parting and heavy Beatles style fringe.

"Glasgow," The young man was softly spoken and seemed ill at ease with the attention.

"Aye I can tell that. Whereabouts?"

"Castlemilk. I went to Our Lady and St. Margaret's."

"Ah fucking hell. Did you know Rab Boyle?" Alan pulled up a chair and sat down and the young men eyed each other nervously.

"No I don't think so." The young man took a sip of his orange juice.

"You know the CYC? The Castlemilk Young Craig? Rab was one of their top boys...did you ever run with a team yourself?"

"No, I stayed away from all that. I just played football, that's all." The young men exchanged furtive glances and one reached over and picked up his jacket.

"Oh come on boys, you're not away so soon? Norman's just getting us some drinks. What's your name anyway pal?" Alan extended his hand as Wesley and Scotty sat down.

"Edwin Gray. My mates call me Eddie."

"Pleased to meet you Eddie. You going to be playing in the semi-final then?"

"No, I've not played for the first team yet, hopefully soon. Jimmy here has though, and Peter's played once too..." Eddie nodded across at a thin youth with a gap in his teeth who smiled back nervously.

"Thought you might have all got a game last night against Burnley with it being 'second game in three days?" Wesley pulled up a stool and sat down.

"Mr Revie doesn't like to change a winning team."

"Are you from Glasgow too Pete?" Alan accepted a coke from Norman and swigged it from the bottle.

"Dundee."

"Ah well hard luck. At least you're not fucking English anyway eh?" Alan leant over and slapped the young man on the back, causing him to lurch forward.

"Anyways, I've got a proposition for you boys." The young men looked nervous as Alan stood up.

"Do you like my suit? Two tone mohair. Made to measure. You know how much a suit like this costs?"

Eddie Gray shrugged "Billy just had one made at Austin Reed. I think it was just less than twenty pounds."

"Sounds about right and I'll bet it's not the same quality as ours." Alan held out an outstretched palm and Scotty, Norman and Wesley patted down their suit jackets. Non-Stop Nigel stared at a caged parrot which was swearing at customers queuing for coffee.

"How would you like to own suits like these boys?"

"I'm still on apprentice wages." Eddie shook his head.

"Well, I can help you out there." Alan sat down again and leant in close to Eddie, beckoning Peter towards him. The blond youth sipped his coke, eyes flickering nervously.

"I can get all three of you a suit like this for nothing...well, for no cash."

The three young footballers continued to exchange nervous glances as Alan continued with his pitch.

"No cash required...what I do need is semi-final tickets."

"Five tickets? We're only getting two each so I'm..." Edwin Gray was shaking his head.

"No, no, no. Elaine here has managed to sort us out with tickets for ourselves. I'm talking about a business transaction. I've got the contacts around town and I'm guessing you could get hold of the tickets. 50/50 on the profit and I'll also sort you boys out with some nice suits."

"No, I'm sorry, as I said we're only getting a couple each anyway." Eddie caught Peter's eye and he signalled with a flick of the head that it was time to go.

"What about the first team though? They'll be getting loads surely. Any of your pals in the team that you can put me in touch with? What about wee Billy?" Alan grabbed hold of his arm as Eddie stood up.

"I'm sorry, no. We've only got 200 for all the players, directors and sponsors. FA Rules, so the first team don't have enough either." The blond boy stood up and passed Eddie his overcoat as Alan got up from his seat, blocking Peter's exit route.

"What about pills? Uppers...they'll make you run faster." Alan reached into his jacket pocket and produced a plastic bag filled with French blues. Peter shook his head and stepped backwards.

"Alan, no, stop it, leave them alone." Elaine pushed Alan's hand away angrily and stood between him and the players who mumbled their goodbyes and hastily pulled on their coats.

"Come on boys, this is a great opportunity!" Alan shouted after the players as they shuffled up the three steps towards the dance floor and the exit doors.

"For God's sake Alan! Wesley, you didn't tell me that's why you were coming here..." Elaine shook her head, her Kohl-coated eyes flashing angrily.

"I didn't know myself." Wesley shrugged as Alan returned to the table shaking his head.

"Fuck's sake. A cup semi-final is a massive opportunity to make some serious money. Money that we wouldn't need to hand over to Donovan. Come on Elaine, you must be able to get hold of more tickets?"

"I can't. I told you. I've had to call in all sorts of favours to get you four."

"I can imagine what the favour was for that Greenhoff kid." Norman grinned, Scotty laughed and Wesley scowled.

"Piss off Norman. Jimmy's just a nice lad. There's nowt like that going on." Elaine folded her arms and looked down at the square toes of her granny shoes.

"I've got it! You leave a window unlocked at the ticket office and we'll break in and nick the tickets." Alan was pacing, bottle of coke in hand.

"Do you think they're just going to be lying around on 'desk? We haven't even got them yet and when we do they'll be kept in 'safe. I take it you're a safe cracker Alan?"

"Fucking hell. This is a big opportunity missed boys, a chance to get some proper cash behind us." Alan sat down rubbing his chin as he stared at the ceiling, his feet resting on the table, tapping to the beat of 'Baby Please Don't Go.'

A sudden clap of Elaine's hands caused all the lads to turn towards her.

"I've just had a thought." Her white lipstick cracked into a wide smile.

"Go on..." Alan stood and faced her.

"Tokens." Elaine was smirking now, nodding her head.

"What's that mean?" Alan leant in closer.

"That's how you get tickets. Tokens from 'programme. We're getting 21,000 tickets for Hillsborough. 5000 for season ticket holders then the rest go on sale on Wednesday. They're staggering it so if you've got 24 tokens you can queue from 10 o'clock. Then if you've got 20 tokens it's midday. Then if there's any tickets left, they're selling to people with 16 tokens from 3 o'clock."

"So?" Alan was failing to see the opportunity.

"So...if you've got 24 tokens you're guaranteed a ticket. It's not tickets you need to be getting hold of, it's tokens. People will buy tokens from you, because tokens get you tickets." Elaine looked pleased with herself and took a swig of her coke float.

"But we haven't got any of these fucking tokens have we?" Alan threw up his hands and shook his head.

"Ah, but this is where some inside knowledge comes in!" Elaine tapped the side of her nose. "Because I know a place where you can get hold of as many tokens as you want!"

Chapter 16

"It looks really smart, I've never seen a suit that colour." Christine Harrison leant on the counter of La Conca d'Ora coffee bar as Alan Connolly took a backwards step and patted his lapels.

"You won't see another like it. One of a kind. See the vent? I made all the other lads get side vents, but in London now it's all centre vents, so that's what I went for. Guess how many inches?"

Christine shook her head. "Eighteen?"

"Twenty! Twenty fucking inches...sorry." Alan put his hand over his mouth and felt his face flush.

"The old guy who made it said he'd never done a twenty-inch vent in his life! It's waisted and obviously there's no shoulder pads. Open cuff with a link button. 15-inch bottoms on the trousers."

"Looks great!" Christine fiddled with the button on the bottle green mac she'd bought at Chelsea Girl on Boar Lane specially for her date, as Alan opened his jacket to show off his shirt.

"Button-down, pastel blue, I got a green one too. The tie is knitted, Madras cotton. Cost 12/6."

"You look really smart." Alan was suddenly conscious that he hadn't stopped talking since he'd arrived, and he wondered if he could sense a hint of disappointment in her voice.

"Oh, sorry, you look great too!" It had been so long since he'd spoken properly to a girl. *Fucking idiot. Stop talking so fast.*

"Thanks, it's just some old stuff." She looked down at the Hush Puppies and men's straight-leg hipster trousers like the ones Cathy McGowan had been wearing on Ready Steady Go. Her mum had wanted her to wear her M&S A-line skirt but it was a couple of inches too short now. Just below the knee was 'in' this month.

"Where shall we go? Del Rio?"

Alan shook his head. "There's a band on at the BG tonight, the Graham Bond Organisation. Norman says they're touring with Chuck Berry this year. Fancy that?"

"Anywhere...yeah, fab!" Christine smiled.

Out onto the rain lashed cobbles of Upper Mill Hill, Alan holding the door as they left the Conc.

"What do you..? Have you been..?" Their words collided in a failed attempt to avoid an awkward silence, and they both laughed, then stuttered as they tried to avoid a repetition.

"Your job then...what do you do?" Christine managed to speak first.

"Security stuff. We look after businesses around town."

"Sounds interesting. Better than working in Woolworths like me."

"Aye, well, I've just started, but I've got lots of ideas. That's important. You can always get by without money but not without ideas."

"That's a good saying. Who came up with that?"

"I heard it in...somewhere...can't think where now." Alan smiled and Christine laughed and put her arm through his, which made his heart leap in his chest.

They reached Boar Lane and turned left past Jacomelli's, crossing the road towards White Horse Street. The damp March air still held the chill of a Yorkshire winter, and Christine tightened her grip on his arm and moved closer to him as they dodged a passing black taxi to cross the road.

Entering the dark cobbled street opposite Trinity Church, the sound of muffled voices caused them to look left, to see the wide white eyes of a man illuminated in a torch beam. Slumped on the floor, he looked up at two dark figures standing above him in the darkness. Alan and Christine paused as one of the figures raised his foot and brought it down hard onto the side of the man's face.

The prone figure screamed in pain and Alan stopped, the scuffling of his feet on the cobbles causing the two figures to turn towards them. The silver on the helmet badge made Alan's pulse quicken, and he urged Christine forward.

"Come on, they're police. Leave them to it." *Keep your head down.*

Christine hesitated at the sound of the man on the floor sobbing.

"Please, no, leave me. I'll move on. No problem, please." Alan could see now that the cowering figure on the floor was a black man in his early thirties, wearing a soiled grey overcoat.

"What's wrong with him?" Christine pulled away from Alan and slowly walked towards the men.

"He's drunk love. Causing problems. Nothing to concern yourself with." The officer leered as he looked Christine up and down, ignoring Alan standing behind her.

"Please lady, help me. They'll kill me, please help..." The man raised his hands, imploring Christine to help. *The coppers down here are cunts.*

"Come on, he's just a tramp, we shouldn't get involved..." Alan took her arm and tried to lead her away.

"We can't leave him." Christine stepped forward between the two officers and crouched beside the man, who had a large cut on the side of his forehead.

"Please, please...please help me." Tears poured down the man's cheeks and Christine took his hand and turned towards Alan.

"Help me get him up."

"You'll need to disinfect yourselves now you've touched him," one of the policemen smirked as Alan hauled the man to his feet.

"Go on pal, get on your way." Alan picked up a bottle-filled carrier bag from the doorway and handed it to the dishevelled black man, who limped towards the lights of Boar Lane.

"Scottish..." The other officer stood in Alan's way.

"Aye."

"What brings you to Leeds then?" He flicked the beam of his torch onto Alan's face, causing him to flinch and turn away.

"My brother plays for Leeds, I'm down for a visit, hoping to see the semi-final too."

The officers looked at each other and nodded their approval.

"Who's your brother then son?"

"Billy Bremner." He was the only Scottish player Alan could recall and it clearly had the desired effect as the officers smiled and the one with the torch turned it off.

"That's great, you don't look much like him though?"

"Nah he takes after our Ma, I take after our dad with the dark hair you see..."

"Any chance of a ticket for the semi then?" The officers were all smiles as Alan turned away, steering Christine towards the door of the BG.

"I'll see what I can do lads!" He waved a goodbye and crooked his left arm, waiting for her touch, which never came. She remained silent until they reached the doorway.

"Billy Bremner?" A quizzical, raised eyebrow suggested suspicion, disappointment, maybe anger. Alan knew for certain though that it hadn't taken her long to work one thing out for certain. *You're a fucking liar Alan.*

Chapter 17

Wednesday 17 March 1965

*Luther King Urges New March on Courthouse -
Montgomery (Alabama) - Dr. Martin Luther King,
Negro Civil rights leader, has called for negroes and
whites to march on the courthouse here today to
demand an apology for police actions against
demonstrators yesterday. In yesterday's clash, eight
people, including a white professor from Pennsylvania
and two negro girl students were taken to hospital after
sheriff's deputies on horses beat demonstrators with
clubs and whips.*

"Norman – you go first, you probably had the toughest
patch up the top end of town." Alan Connolly took a sip
from his mug then placed it on the table in the Del Rio
coffee bar and picked up a pad and a pen.

Norman squinted at a scrap of paper he'd produced from
his pocket.

"Number 18 Coffee Bar on Eastgate, nowt. Pop-In Cafe,
nowt, but I called into 'Smith and Nelson's snooker hall
next door and shifted a dozen blues and five bombers to
some rockers."

"Good lad. Initiative. I like that." Alan nodded his
approval as he scribbled in the pad.

"Carousel, thirty, all blues. Miami, two dozen blues to
some nurses from 'LGI. Riviera, nowt. Best one was
'Flamenco opposite 'Grand. There were a group of
foreign blokes in, Italians or summat, probably waiters

and I'm sure they were poofters. Anyway they bought a dozen blues each."

Alan's eyes lit up. "How many's that?"

"There were seven of them, so I shifted eighty four to them and another ten to an older couple who were dancing to James Brown on' Juke Box."

"That's good work for midweek. Any more?"

"Nowt in 'Hellenic or Kardomah, but I also managed to shift thirty reds. So that's me." Norman screwed up the piece of paper and put in his mouth. The others stared at him.

"Evidence." he winked.

"Go on then Wes, let's have yours." Alan nodded across the table and Wesley produced a betting slip from his jacket pocket.

"I didn't break it down like Norman. I've just got a total."

"For fuck's sake Wesley, I told you I want to know what we're shifting and where, especially at the bottom end of town. Do it right next time. So where did you go and what did you sell?" Alan jabbed the pencil in Wesley's direction causing him to puff out his cheeks and exhale loudly.

"Okay, Four Cousins, La Staega, Tropica, El Toro, American Bar, the Conc, Three Coins and the BG..." he paused, waiting for Alan to stop writing in his pad.

"Go on then, how many?"

"168 blues, 34 bombers, 42 Dexes, 40 reds. Plus some Mary-Jane I got from Black Anthony."

"Good numbers but don't be running any fucking side deals Wes. Mr Donovan has his own pot outlets. That's not our business."

"Wasn't much, just some I had left..."

"I don't fucking care! You don't sell it again...understood?" Alan's voice caused the lads to sit up straight around the table.

"Understood." Wesley mumbled a response and shrugged.

"Okay Scotty, how'd you do with the older crowd?"

"I feel like I've walked ten miles. I must have been in every pub and club in town. If I told you all the ones I sold nowt in I'd be here all night." Scotty grimaced and rubbed at his calves.

"Go on then, numbers." Alan was poised with his pen.

"I haven't split them down into types but...King Charles 60, Whitelocks 28, Peel 88, Aloha at Jacomelli's 24, Piccadilly 18, Keyhole Club, nowt, hardly anyone in, probably too early. Ioanna's was quiet but I sold two dozen to the bouncer, no doubt he'll sell them on."

"Well fuck that, who's he think he is? Tell him you do the selling and if he doesn't like it, I'll be round to discuss it with him." Alan closed his pad and put it in his jacket pocket, then checked his watch.

"That's not too bad for a Wednesday boys, and the night is still young. Steam Packet are on at the BG, should be a good crowd. Let's go make some more money boys!"

Chapter 18

Alan saw her as soon as he descended the steps towards the dancefloor of the BG club. Not that anyone could miss her. Crouching on her haunches in front of the hardboard DJ stand perched on the tiny stage, she rocked back and forth to the beat of the Stones 'Last Time', her long dark hair sweeping the dancefloor, before springing to her feet, eyes cast to the ceiling as if transfixed by the crude strobe lighting rig. Arms extended, she then seemed bewildered by the movement of her own fingers as she cast shapes in the darkness, her eyes wide and mouth contorted in apparent ecstasy.

"Jesus, what a nutcase. She hasn't got any shoes on." Wesley watched the girl with a furrowed brow.

"I've never seen anyone dance like that before." Norman shook his head as the girl noticed them on the stairs and pointed, before tossing her head back and cackling like a crazed witch.

Alan stepped back as she approached, first turning her back then rubbing herself against him while running her fingers through her matted hair.

"Dance with me." She grabbed Alan's hand but he pulled away, embarrassed as his mates started laughing.

"Looks like she fancies you boss." Wesley laughed as the DJ changed the record and 'Shop Around' crackled through the speakers.

"Sapphire." Alan hadn't noticed the young man approach to stand next to him on the steps.

"You what?" Alan took a sideways step to assess the man. Late twenties, small and slight with thick, collar length hair and a purple velvet jacket over a yellow polo neck. *Fucking Beatnik.*

"Sapphire. Her name is Sapphire. Or that's what she says anyway." The young man smiled as the girl skipped around the dancefloor, tossing imaginary flowers over the few dancing couples trying hard to avoid her.

"Is she your girl then?" Alan had to stoop to make himself heard above the music.

"She lives with me, but she's not my girl. I don't think she's ever been anyone's girl. She's what you call a free spirit. American you see."

"I've never met an American." Alan clenched his fist as soon as the words had left his mouth. *What a fucking stupid thing to say. Think before you speak.*

The young man didn't seem to hear though as his eyes remained on the dancing girl.

"I'm Stanley. Stanley Mortimer." He extended his hand.

"Alan Connolly." Alan reached out and squeezed too hard, watching Stanley Mortimer flinch. "Want some pills? I run all the stuff around here."

The young man barely reacted and shook his head.

"Prefer some Mary Jane? That's what you lot like isn't it?"

"And who are 'my lot' exactly?" Stanley Mortimer smiled, his eyes suggesting amusement rather than annoyance.

"Beats. I assumed that's what you were?"

The young man sniffed. "Beatniks, mods, rockers. Why do people always need to apply labels to others?"

"Aye you're right. Stupid names. I don't even call myself a mod anymore. I'm a stylist."

"There you go again." Alan didn't hear Stanley Mortimer's response as Sapphire reeled across the dancefloor towards them and took hold of Stanley's hands while staring hard into Alan's eyes.

"More medicine daddy." Her words were just audible above Smokey Robinson's urging to 'get yourself a bargain son.'

"You're a naughty girl." Stanley Mortimer reached into the top pocket of his velvet jacket and withdrew a chemical dropper, which he flicked twice as Sapphire leant backwards, mouth open wide. He then squeezed the rubber teat onto the girl's outstretched tongue, causing her to squeal with delight then spin and reel across the dancefloor.

"Want some?" Stanley Mortimer paused and turned to Alan before placing the dropper back in his pocket.

"What is it?" Alan regarded the dropper with suspicion.

"Acid."

"She's drinking fucking acid?" Alan's eyes widened.

"Not that type of acid." Mortimer tipped his head back and squeezed the dropper into his own mouth then extended his arm, suspending it directly in Alan's eyeline. Alan glanced to his left and saw Norman and Wesley looking on as Scotty returned from the bar with a handful of coke bottles.

Alan opened his mouth and felt the liquid on his tongue.

"What's it do?"

"Wait and see. If you like it, come and see me tomorrow."
Stanley Mortimer tore a page out of a pocket diary and
thrust it into the top pocket of Alan's jacket, beckoned
Sapphire from the dance floor and turned to leave.

"Enjoy your trip, Alan Connolly."

Chapter 19

Open wide. Needles on his tongue.

Eyes wide. Eyes closed.

Tobacco and whiskey.

The monster smiling. The monster laughing.

Shit and piss.

Making him gag, making him choke.

Vomit on his tongue. Tears on his cheek.

Stop ya greeting, ya wee poofter.

Eyes open, father smiling, father laughing.

Brush in his hand. Paper and piss.

Needles on his tongue. Tears on his cheek.

Eyes closed, mouth wide.

Father laughing, Alan crying. Alan dying.

Never safe again.

Chapter 20

Thursday 18 March 1965

Walk in Space - 300 Miles up...just a line from eternity, Alexei does Somersault- Three hundred miles above the earth a man goes for a 20 minute 'walk' and does somersaults. This stranger-than-fiction happening - man's first ever venture outside an orbiting spaceship, was part of a Russian space spectacular today. Millions of Russians watching the space show on TV gasped as cosmonaut Colonel Alexei Leonov (30) emerged slowly from the spaceship Voskhod (Sunrise) II, climbing slowly into space, making swimming motions and pulling on a lifeline connecting him with the ship. All the time, Voskhod II was spinning through space at 5 miles per second.

"So you're a doctor then?" Alan Connolly stared from the window of the terraced flat in Kensington Terrace, Hyde Park. He tried to focus on two schoolboys admiring the Lambretta parked on the cobbled street, but his attention was repeatedly drawn to the reflection of Sapphire walking naked from the kitchen to the living room, a cannabis cigarette suspended between her lips.

"A chemist, yes. I'm working on a project at the university." Stanley Mortimer reclined on a sofa, extending his right arm to receive the joint.

"A chemist? Like Boots?" Alan turned back to face the room, desperately trying to maintain eye contact with the pale faced young man who seemed amused by his presence.

"Not quite Alan no. My last employer was actually the U.S. Government. I don't suppose you've heard of MK-Ultra? Project Bluebird? Project Artichoke?"

Alan shook his head as Stanley drew on the cigarette.

"Sidney Gottlieb...Alan Dulles? You must have heard of the CIA?"

"Erm...I've heard of C&A, the shop..."

Mortimer roared with laughter and Alan felt the knot tighten in his stomach as his face reddened.

"Bloody hell Alan, you're a funny old cat!" Stanley Mortimer passed the joint back to Sapphire, and she slowly approached Alan, who breathed hard as he fought to avoid staring down at the dark triangle between her legs.

"Have you heard of Harvard?" Mortimer didn't wait for an answer. "It's a university in America. The U.S. Government sent me there to work with a couple of psychology lecturers, Leary and Alpert, who were conducting experiments with a substance called Lysergic Acid Diethylmide. The government, and the military in particular, were interested to know whether LSD, or acid as we call it, could be developed as a truth drug. I was top of my class at Cambridge, and they sent me in, undercover, as it were, to spy on them."

Alan was aware of Sapphire swaying in front of him, but fixed his gaze on Mortimer over her shoulder until she took his hand and pulled him towards her. Alan tried to speak but almost immediately her lips were on his, wet and tasting of cherry and tobacco. She opened her mouth and filled his with cannabis smoke. Alan took a step back as she giggled and turned away.

Back on the sofa, Stanley Mortimer didn't seem to have noticed his girlfriend kissing their visitor even though he was still staring at Alan.

"I spent two years with them, working on concepts such as ego dissolution – the complete loss of subjective identity. I came to understand that the answer to all the world's problems lies within the framework of analytic psychology, sometimes referred to as Jungian analysis, and specifically the possibility of complete ego death..."

"Can I plate you Alan?" Sapphire was stood in the middle of the room facing him.

"Beg your pardon? What?" Alan's heart felt like it was about to explode from his chest as she slowly approached him and began fumbling with his belt. *Sin and depravity, all about you.*

"In death and rebirth mythology, ego death is the ultimate phase of self surrender...She wants to suck your John Thomas old chap, in California they call it 'plating', Lord knows why...anyway, ego death is a recurrent theme in ancient mythology and is also used as a metaphor in some strands of western cultural thinking...."

Alan's gaze remained focused on Stanley Mortimer as his suit trousers fell to his ankles, followed by his Y-fronts, and Sapphire sank to her knees in front of him.

"Ego death can be temporarily replicated in the form of ego dissolution, following ingestion of certain plant derived substances, such as peyote or ayahuasca, and the research we carried out at Harvard led me to understand..."

Stanley Mortimer's words became nothing more than distorted noise as Alan stared fixedly out of the window, with only an occasional downward glance at Sapphire's head, rising and falling over his groin. Treading a mental tightrope between euphoria and trauma, his mind was flooded with contrasting suggestions of escape, sexual fulfilment and violence.

He slowly raised his right hand to feel the shape of the bayonet in the lining of his jacket, his heart rate slowing, his breathe feeling calmer as he squeezed the hard steel. *Breathe slowly. In control. I can do anything, anything I choose.*

Chapter 21

"Cup of tea anyone?" The appearance of Stanley Mortimer's head round the bedroom door caused Alan to tug the covers up over his bare chest.

"Erm...no, not for me thanks."

"Come and join us honey." Sapphire lifted her head from the pillow and stretched out her arms.

"I'm busy darling. You have fun." Stanley blew a kiss and closed the door.

"Doesn't he mind?" Alan sat up in the bed.

"Mind what?" Sapphire rested her head on the pillow and gently tousled his hair with her left hand.

"You screwing with me...doesn't he mind?"

"Why would he mind? He doesn't own me Alan!" She laughed and ran her fingers through her hair.

"Well I wouldn't like it."

"Oh Alan. You're so funny. So hung up on convention."

"What's that mean?"

Sapphire giggled as she propped herself up on her elbow.

"You're such a square. You allow your life to be ruled by convention and fear of consequence. You don't live in the moment."

"I'm not a square..."

"You are though. You're a square and you're scared. I can see your shadow.

"Shadow?" Alan looked around the room.

"Yeah, you have a dark shadow. The shadow of your ego."

"I don't know what the fuck you're talking about." Alan's response caused Sapphire to laugh out loud again.

"What's important to you? Right now...what do you think about when you wake up of a morning?"

Alan sighed and looked up to the high ceiling of the Victorian apartment.

"Plans...Business...making money." *I'm a man with a plan.*

"Okay...why? Why is that important?"

"Because I want to be someone...be something. Someone people look up to."

"But why is that important to you?"

Alan considered the question and shook his head, then pushed back the blanket and swung his legs from the bed.

"Because I don't want to end up like my Da.." *Plan for the future or return to your past.*

"Your father? Why?"

"Fucking questions...why are you asking me all these questions?" Alan put his hands on his head and walked to the window, peering out from behind the net curtains. *Switch flicked, hum of the electrical current filling his head.*

"Because it's important...and I like you."

Alan turned away from the window and stooped to pick up his Y-Fronts.

"Because I fucking hate the cunt, that's why."

"Your father? Okay, that's good. Carry on..."

"He ruined my fucking life. Made our lives a misery...and he killed my Ma. Is that good enough for you?"

Alan fought back tears as he began to pull on his trousers, facing away from the girl on the bed. *Electricity surging, the humming in his head becoming a deafening buzz.*

"Metaphorically killed your mother or...you mean he actually killed your mother?" Sapphire was sat up in bed now.

"Stabbed her to death. I was eight."

"Oh shit. I'm sorry Alan...wow, that's heavy."

"Stabbed her when she tried to stop him drowning his wee son one Saturday afternoon."

"You...? You were the boy?"

Alan's bare chest heaved visibly as he nodded and fought back tears. *Tobacco and whiskey. The monster smiling.*

"Aye. He tried to drown me in the bath. She fought him off and he killed her. She died saving my life. So do you understand now why I hate him, why I have to be better than him? Prove to myself that I'm not like him?"

Sapphire stood and walked around the bed, placing her right hand gently on his left shoulder as she looked into his eyes.

"I get it, of course I do, but you can't let your father define you. You have to let go."

"Let go? Of what?"

"Of the past. Of your fear...your ego. We can help you."

"Who's we?" Alan pulled away and picked up his shirt from the floor.

"Stanley and I, we can help. We can help you to transition your psyche, to reshape your identity, beliefs, and emotions. Lose those memories of what happened when you were a kid. You can learn to fly. That's what he did for me in South America."

"You've been to South America?"

"Yeah, I was living in Zihuatanejo in Mexico when Stanley moved there with Leary and Alpert after Harvard sacked them. They hooked up with two guys, Ginsberg and Burroughs who'd been experimenting with a plant called ayuhuasca since '53. We travelled to the Amazon together, met a shaman, Kacha, one hundred and twenty years old, he taught us so much, and he conducted the chupada where my old self died and I was reborn."

"I've not got a fucking clue what any of that means..." Alan was buttoning up his shirt as the door opened and Stanley Mortimer silently entered the room and sat cross legged on the floor.

"Honey, I was just telling Alan how we can help him to shed his ego, take away his dark shadow and rebirth him."

"How did you enjoy your trip last night Alan?" Stanley placed his hands together and positioned them under his chin, as if in prayer.

"Aye, it was alright. Made the music sound amazing and the shitty lights in the BG looked like shooting stars. No good for dancing though, it felt like I was walking on jelly. My mates pissed themselves laughing."

"Dreams?"

Alan hesitated. *Tobacco and whiskey. The monster smiling.*

 "No I don't think so."

"Because if you're in the wrong frame of mind, maybe weighed down by thoughts of the past, it's all too easy to slip into a bad trip."

"Stanley has studied the Bardo Thodol, the Tibetan Book of the Dead. It's so cool Alan. He can help you escape your shadow, just like he did for me." Sapphire joined Stanley on the floor and began stroking his hair.

"Yeah thanks, I'll think about it...There was one thing I was wondering?" Alan put on his jacket and fastened only the top button of the three, the mod way.

"Ask away." Stanley rested his head on Sapphire's shoulder and she closed her eyes.

"What would happen if you were to mix this acid of yours with another drug, like speed for instance?"

Stanley Mortimer smiled. "Ah yes, you mod types and your Purple Hearts..."

"There are no Hearts now, it's French Blues."

"Drynamil. Same thing... Well, the first problem you'll have is that your pills are coated so they dissolve in your stomach not in your mouth. That means they wouldn't absorb the acid. If you could get over that though...it could be an interesting experiment." Stanley nodded encouragingly.

"So cut them in half." Sapphire's eyes were still closed.

"In half?"

"Well I guess they're only coated on the outside...so cut them in half, and the middle will absorb the acid, won't it?"

Stanley and Alan exchanged glances.

"Certainly worth a go. Come on." The chemist pulled himself to his feet and pointed the way towards the kitchen. Sapphire took Alan's hand and they followed behind, his brain wrestling with the economics of a stronger dose and a higher price from only half a pill. *Switch flicked, electrical charge crackling and buzzing. Fuck you Clive Donovan. Fuck you Frankie Fields. I'm a man with a plan.*

Chapter 22

"Like a purple diamond." Stanley Mortimer held the tweezers up to the light from the kitchen window and Sapphire and Alan narrowed their eyes to stare at the half tablet being rotated before them.

"It's more navy blue than purple," Alan observed the colour changing as the acid penetrated the pill's coating.

"Not a diamond. A teardrop." Sapphire smiled and extended her index finger and thumb, to gently remove the tablet from the tweezers. She held it to the light again and tilted it back and forth, then slowly placed it upon her tongue and swallowed.

"Purple Hearts, Black Bombers, French Blues... All good products need a brand nowadays." Alan looked on as Sapphire closed her eyes and danced into the centre of the room, swaying slowly in time to a scratchy copy of 'The Pushers' by Dizzy Gillespie, revolving on a turntable in the corner.

"Purple Teardrops?"

Sapphire giggled at Alan's suggestion as she ran her hands through her hair.

"No...I'm already starting to feel the hit from this. You made some good stuff here baby..."

"Why thank you." Stanley Mortimer leant on the window sill as he watched Sapphire bend and sway to the music.

"Oh yeah...you invented something groovy...something wild...dangerous. It's taking me back to my rebirth, back into the jungle...back to where it all began again."

Sapphire closed her eyes and moved her head slowly in time to the measured backbeat of the music.

"I can hear the Shaman's song, the Icaro....so beautiful...I can feel that emotion again honey....I can hear Kacha crying...that's what you made baby...you made...Kacha's Teardrops."

Chapter 23

"Halves? Who's going to buy halves?" Norman held the tiny half tablet to the light of the window in Alan's flat.

"No one." Alan took the pill from him and held it in front of his face. "Open wide."

Norman opened his mouth while glancing at the TV set, where Valerie Singleton was hand painting a hardboiled egg on Blue Peter. Alan placed the pill onto his tongue.

"No one will buy them, because we're going to be giving them away."

"Eh? For free? You've lost me boss." Scotty shook his head as he considered the small dark blue shape in his palm.

"We'll give the first ones away as free samples with the rest of the stuff we sell. I've a feeling that by next week, no one will want anything else."

"How many are there?" Scotty tipped a handful from a polythene bag into his hand.

"I split three hundred pills so there's six hundred. The Outer Limits are on at the BG, and Zoot Money is at the Coins tonight so town will be busy."

"Mr Donovan won't be happy if he hears about this." Wesley leant back on the couch and puffed out his cheeks, exhaling loudly.

"Well he won't fucking hear about it will he? As long as we sell the same number of pills as usual, he won't know any different, but we'll be making twice the profit, or more. This is our chance to make some proper money boys. Then when we've done that and everyone's heard about our teardrops, we can start buying the speed wholesale, cut Donovan out altogether." Alan pulled on his parka and stood in the kitchen doorway.

"Yeah but Father Ernest has eyes everywhere, if he finds...."

"For fucks sake Wesley! I don't want to hear about Father Ernest or Donovan. If you don't like it, you can fuck off." Alan's raised voice caused the other three youths to glance nervously at each other.

"Are you with me or not?" Alan stood in the doorway and looked at each of them in turn, taking their silence as acceptance of the plan.

"Good. Come on, let's get out and give Leeds its first taste of Kacha's Teardrops!"

Chapter 24

Alan had heard 'Not Fade Away' a thousand times, but he'd never appreciated the clarity and range of Jagger's vocals, the sheer anarchy of Brian Jones' harmonica, or Wyman's driving bass which now seemed to be emanating from deep within him.

He'd danced to the song dozens of times, but he'd never danced like this. Filled with an explosive energy which seemed to drive him at warp speed, he could feel the electrical current coursing through his veins, powering his muscles, allowing him to twist and contort his body as if his bones had become elastic. Looking down, his elastic-side Cuban-heel boots no longer even touched the gum-scarred dancefloor, they now levitated on a bed of air, lifting him above the other dancers. *You can learn to fly.*

And the speakers at the BG club didn't crackle and buzz tonight, the lights didn't flicker and dim. Strobe lights flashed, illuminating a hundred smiling faces who looked skywards to see not the low, sweat-stained ceiling but a multi-coloured constellation of planets and stars, shining and blinking in perfect time to the music. *Wired right tonight.*

The DJ flipped the disc and Heatwave burst from the speakers causing the whole crowd to raise their arms and sing...*whenever I'm with you.* Eyes wide, faces flushed, mouths open, grinning, laughing, chewing. The whole room seemed infused with a delirium, an appreciation of a moment that would never be forgotten. Never be repeated.

Alan spotted Christine and Elaine on the edge of the dancefloor and pushed his way through the spinning, heaving mass of dancers towards them.

"You dancing?" He grabbed Christine by the hand and pulled her to the centre of the room.

"Wow, look at you. Look at everyone. It's crazy in here tonight." She laughed as Elaine appeared alongside them with Wesley, grinning and spinning like a top.

Alan reached into his breast pocket and produced a half pill, holding it in front of Christine's mouth.

"No, I don't take owt like that. Ciggies are enough for me."

"Come on, just try it, for me." He kissed her on the lips but Christine pushed his hand away.

"Come on, it will make you dance as good as me." Alan pulled his jacket from his shoulders and began strutting like Mick Jagger, puffing up his lips and pouting.

Norman and Scotty appeared, both sweating and smiling.

"Fuck me Alan, what's in these pills? It's fucking amazing." Scotty was swaying from side to side, pointing at the ceiling. "Look at those coloured circles."

"How many did you give out?" The record changed again and Alan's head was nodding so fast to 'King of Kings' by Jimmy Cliff that his eyes were unable to focus.

"All of them. People have been coming back begging for more, even offering to pay. When can we get some more?"

Alan looked over his shoulder at Christine dancing with Elaine and Wesley, then leaned in close, cupping his hand to shout into Scotty's ear.

"Should have a new batch tomorrow. We won't be taking any though. We've got a job to do."

Chapter 25

Friday 19 March 1965

Arthington Prepares to Join Ghost Stations -Along with other stations on the picturesque Leeds (City)- Ilkley line, Arthington station goes under the Beeching axe on Sunday. Arthington's three waiting rooms, ladies room and passenger subway will still echo to the clackety-clack of train wheels after Sunday, because the Leeds-Harrogate line will still be operative, but trains will no longer stop there. On some of the 22 stopping trains which currently use Arthington each day, it's possible to travel as far afield as Manchester and West Hartlepool without changing. But the handful of passengers who have used the station latterly did not justify its remaining open and it becomes one of seventeen stations in the Leeds Corporation area destined for closure before the end of 1966..

"You sure you haven't been taking teardrops while you were out selling tonight Norman?" Alan shone the torch into the back of the van.

"No, honest, so many people wanted them, I wouldn't even have had one spare even if I'd wanted to. Why?"

"Because you're crashing around a lot back there."

"I've got no choice, this fucking thing has no suspension. Where did you nick it from Scotty, a junk yard?"

"Shut the fuck up, Norman. It's 'biggest van I could find...this is the place here." Scotty peered out of the windscreen at a white sign with blue writing on the side of an industrial unit off Canal Road in Armley.

'J.Rostron and Son, West Leeds Printing Works.'

Alan squinted at his watch in the darkness.

"3am. No lights. Looks like you were right Nigel, and the old codger gets some kip after doing his rounds."

Scotty turned off the engine and Alan gently slid open the van door, then retrieved a Pan-Am holdall from the footwell.

"What did Elaine say we're looking for Wes?"

"She only came once with 'bloke who drops off the unsold programmes. She said it was like a big garage or air raid shelter with wooden doors. That's where they store them before melting them down or summat to use again."

"How do you melt paper?" Norman was sniggering as Alan opened the bag and retrieved a balaclava.

"You all got something to cover your faces, just in case?"

Scotty, Norman and Wesley pulled up their parka hoods and wrapped Leeds scarves around their faces, leaving only their eyes visible. Non-stop Nigel pulled a square of black cloth from his pocket and tied it across the lower half of his face.

"You look like the Lone Ranger Nige...but in a sheepskin coat...what's that for?" Norman shone a torch into the holdall as Alan retrieved a length of washing line and a roll of masking tape.

"In case the old bloke wakes up. We'll need to tie him up." Alan signalled to Norman to switch off the torch and they tiptoed into the car park and past the night watchman's hut.

Turning right around the corner of the red brick industrial unit, Alan raised his arm and the lads stopped behind him to peer into the gloom.

"There, down the far end." Alan whispered and the others followed him along the length of the building to a large shed with an arched, corrugated iron roof and wooden double doors, secured by a padlock.

"Shine the torch on it Norman." The beam flickered in time with Norman's shaking hand as Alan removed a pair of bolt-croppers from the bag and tried to position them to cut the lock."

"They're too big...I can't get a proper hold of it."

"Here let me have a go." Wesley stepped forward and Norman fumbled and dropped the torch which landed on the cobbles with a clatter.

"For fuck's sake Norman!" All heads turned back towards the night watchman's hut, but it remained in darkness.

With the torch beam again focused on the padlock, Wesley struggled to line up the bolt-cutters, and when he finally positioned the blades on to the shank and squeezed the handle grips, the lock remained intact.

"You're not strong enough, you weakling, give it to Nigel."

"Fuck off, I had it then."

"Nigel you have a go."

There were five bodies hunched over the padlock when the powerful torch beam lit them up.

"Who's there? What are you doing? Hey, get away from there!" The voice of an elderly man, his face invisible behind the bright torch light.

"Shit, it's the guard! Run!!" Scotty turned off the torch and was about to make his getaway when Alan grabbed his arm.

"Stop! No one move..."

"I can see you there...the police are coming...get away from there." The light moved forward but there was apprehension in the man's voice now.

"Nigel said he's just an old bloke. We can handle him." Alan sprinted forward towards the light which shook violently and then fell to the floor with a smash, plunging the car park into darkness.

"Come on, help me with him!" Alan's voice was strained as he wrestled with the old man.

"You bastards, I'm not scared of you..I fought in 'first war in 'Pals, you bastards, I'll have you..."

"Nigel hold him down." Scotty shoved the big man forward.

"No names you idiot!" Alan was still rolling on the floor with the guard. "Pass the rope and the tape!"

The night watchman may have been in his late sixties and small in height, but was stocky and strong, and it required a bear-hug from Nigel to subdue him while Scotty bound his arms tightly to his body with the washing line.

"Fuck off, no, no!" The man's face was bloated purple, and veins bulged in his neck and on his forehead as Wesley applied a thick stripe of tape to his mouth. With the struggling guard propped up on a chair in his office and Nigel assigned to keep watch, the others returned to the shed.

Now working with less urgency and with Wesley holding the torch and Norman the padlock, the bolt croppers quickly cut through the shank and the double doors were heaved open and a ceiling striplight flickered to life.

"Oh shit! Look at all this..."

If they'd been expecting racks of unsold Leeds United programmes stacked in chronological order, the contents of the storage unit came as an unwelcome surprise. Row upon row of publications and pamphlets, leaflets and posters of all shapes and sizes were stacked floor to ceiling in jumbled piles.

"This is going to take all night." Norman moaned as they began to investigate seemingly endless rows of returned print jobs waiting to be pulped.

"Jackpot!" After ten minutes of searching, Scotty emerged from a stack of boxes holding a pile of blue and white programmes. "Token number 4, Leeds v Blackpool. There must be three hundred of them."

The others began hauling stacks of paper from racks in the surrounding area and it wasn't long before the search was bearing results.

"Yes!! Two lots here...Token 7, Spurs and 11, West Brom." Wesley's grinning face popped up from behind a pile of paper and cardboard.

"Put them all in here, at this rate we'll be done in a couple of hours." Alan hauled a large packing crate up the aisle and Norman, Scotty and Wesley began to throw bundles of programmes in.

It was 5am, with twelve different sets of tokens secured, when Scotty stopped to stretch his aching back and noticed a large, dark shadow in the doorway.

"Nigel? What's up? Why have you taken your mask off?"

Nigel's face remained impassive. He shook his head and without speaking, turned and left.

"I don't like the look of that," Alan broke into a jog as he set off, following Nigel with the others following.

Nigel had his back to the door as they entered the night watchman's hut, peering over his shoulders towards the chair where the old man, now silent, slumped forward awkwardly.

"What's up with him?" Alan crouched beside the chair and looked up at Nigel who shrugged and shook his head.

"Wake up pal...come on, wakey wakey, time to get up." Alan shook the old man's arm gently to no response.

"How long's he been like this?"

Again, Nigel shrugged, then stepped forward, taking hold of the back of the night watchman's jacket collar to haul him upright.

The old man's head tilted slowly back, and it seemed for a second that he might be about to wake, as he remained upright briefly, but then gravity took effect and he slowly keeled over to the right, taking the chair with him.

The room fell silent as Scotty, Norman and Wesley stared down at the prone figure laying on the floor before them, before turning to stare at Alan, who covered his open mouth with his hand. *Switch flicked, electrical charge humming, buzzing, too loud to think. Fuck.Fuck.Fuck.*

It took a few seconds for anyone to move, before Wesley cautiously crouched on one knee and leant towards the old man's face, purple and bloated. With a tentative hand he reached out to lift one of the guard's eyelids before recoiling, with his hands clasped to his head, to confirm what they all already knew.

"He's dead lads. I think we've killed him."

Chapter 26

Dark. Awake. Walking.

Cold white tiles underfoot.

Sleep in his eyes.

Screaming. Crying.

The monster's voice.

Stop ya greeting, bitch.

Screaming. Crying. Quieter with every kick.

Reaching up. Blue dots on the hand.

Take the hand. The monster's hand.

No more kicks. No more screams.

Blue dots on the fist.

Bright light flashing. Wet face. Warm face.

Black shoe. Red shoe. Red tiles.

Leave the boy. Don't kill the boy.

Screaming. Crying.

'I think we've killed him.'

Chapter 27

Saturday 20 March 1965

Anti-War Slogan Daubed in Leeds Street – 'Vietnam - Stop U.S Murders '- This painted opinion of one of the world's trouble spots has appeared on a wall midway between two main centres of law and order in the city - the new Police headquarters at Brotherton House and the Town Hall. The daubing appeared overnight on Thursday and has not yet been removed. Leeds Corporation Works department said they are aware and will be addressing the vandalism in due course.

"Good result today lads." Alan Connolly opened the door of the flat and Norman, Wesley and Scotty entered silently, their faces a picture of gloom.

"Everton were shit, we should have scored more than four to get our goal average up." Wesley slumped onto the sofa as Scotty removed his Leeds scarf and headed to the kitchen.

"Make us a tea to warm us up Scotty." Norman sunk into the sofa next to Wesley as Alan took up a position on the window sill.

"Have you seen the Green final? Man United lost at Sheffield Wednesday. Good omen for the semi next week." Alan was doing his best to be upbeat, but the dark mood was reflected in his friends' faces.

"Still only two points ahead of Chelsea and they've got a game in hand though." Norman looked at his soaked Clark's Desert Boots and waggled his feet.

"Was there owt in 'paper about...you know what?"

Alan raised his eyebrows.

"You know, last night..." Norman lowered his voice.

"I know what you fucking mean Norman, why are you whispering?"

Norman nervously scanned the room.

"I don't know. What if there's bugs or summat like in 'Man from UNCLE?"

Scotty smirked as he carried three steaming mugs into the room and joined Alan on the window sill.

"I've been thinking about it." Alan stood up and turned to look out of the window at the glow of dusk brake lights approaching Eastgate roundabout. "There's no way to link us to last night and it's unlikely they will, but what if they work out what it was that we nicked...?"

"What? You think they'll notice a load of old programmes missing from all that paper waiting to be pulped?" Wesley was shaking his head.

"As I said, it's unlikely, but you never know. And I've counted up. We've got sets of twelve different programmes. They'll be worth something, but not as much as selling the full twenty you need for a semi-final ticket."

"So?" Wesley scowled and tapped at the side of his mug in anticipation of what was coming.

"So, I don't think it's worth the risk. If word gets out that we've got hold of a load of tokens and someone puts two and two together, we could be in the shit."

"So what are you saying? We don't use them? I know loads of lads who are a few tokens short, they'd pay good money for them."

"As I said, it's not worth the risk. I'm saying we dump them."

"You fucking what? After we nicked a van, robbed a printers and killed someone, you want to bin them?" Wesley stood up, his voice raised and his face flushed.

"We didn't kill him, he must have had a heart attack or something, but that's what I'm saying yes. It's a business decision. The risk outweighs the reward." Alan's voice remained calm but his mind was spinning. *Don't get nicked for anything stupid.*

"Well, you can fuck right off!" Wesley seemed as surprised by his outburst as everyone else in the room, and he stood breathing heavily, his eyes fixed on Alan's.

"We fucking killed an innocent man and you just want to forget the whole thing, so it was all for nowt?. I'll take my share of 'tokens and sell them to lads I know..."

"No you won't. I've made my decision Wes." It was now Alan's turn to raise his voice. "Scotty, you'll burn the programmes when you dump the van."

Scotty nodded and Norman carried on looking at his feet, while Wesley stared out of the window, his shoulders rising and falling visibly, his breathing clearly audible.

"I don't want to hear any more about it. We forget the tokens and move on to something more important." Alan headed into the kitchen and returned with a bulging BOAC holdall which he unzipped, before tipping the contents onto the coffee table. The lads stood and observed the polythene bags and their dark blue contents.

"Teardrops. There's about five hundred here. We'll sell at 2/6 each and see how it goes. If they're shifting, we'll put them up to 3/. Tell people it's still a good deal because one of these is stronger than two blues. And for us, every sale only uses half a pill, so less to pay to Donovan. Clear?"

Scotty and Norman nodded, while Wesley continued to stare silently out of the flat window as Alan continued.

"The even better news is the acid costs next to nothing and my contact can have another batch ready tomorrow, so come on boys, let's get out and get selling. Saturday night, there's a few bands on in town and the weather is starting to pick up. I've got a feeling it's going to be a busy night."

Alan patted Scotty on the back as he followed Norman along the hallway of the flat, then held the door for Wesley who passed without making eye contact.

"Wes..."

Wesley paused but didn't turn to face Alan.

"The old bloke just died. We didn't kill him."

Wesley shrugged and carried on walking, his words lost in the breeze blowing a vortex of crisp packets along the uncovered Quarry Hill landing.

"What's the difference? He's still dead."

Chapter 28

"All sold by ten o'clock, and I sold most of them for 3/."
Norman removed his pork-pie hat, mopped his brow and
took a swig from a bottle of coke.

"What about you two?" Alan raised his voice to be heard
above a sketchy version of Chuck Berry's 'Promised Land'
being belted out by the lead singer of The Dawnbreakers
from the small stage of the Three Coins.

"Same here. Everybody was asking for teardrops, so I
went straight to 3/ and people would have probably paid
more. I've got loads of orders for when we get some
more." Scotty smiled as he nodded his head to the music.

Wesley was silently observing the movement on the
small dancefloor.

"Wes? Did you shift all yours?" Alan nudged his arm.

"Yeah. All gone." He replied while continuing to look
straight ahead.

"Great, how much did you get for them?"

"I charged 2/6, like you said." Scotty and Norman
exchanged glances as Alan stared at Wesley, his jaw
moving mechanically as he worked the gum in his
mouth.

"Okay." Alan turned and faced the dance floor,
drumming an upturned coke bottle on the palm of his
left hand.

Without speaking again, Wesley moved across the dancefloor to greet Elaine and Christine who were passing their coats to the cloakroom attendant.

"Yeah Yeah, Georgie Fame, got to dance to this." Norman re-positioned his hat and strode onto the dancefloor, his arms swinging high in a marching motion.

"It's jumping tonight, look at everyone, totally blocked! You coming?" Scotty didn't wait for an answer as he followed Norman, but Alan remained still, letting the music wash over him as the teardrops began to take effect.

Time seemed to become elastic as the DJ replaced the band and Alan observed the scene from the edge of the dancefloor. It first seemed that Tommy Tucker's 'Hi Heel Sneakers' had been playing for at least an hour, before 'Needle in a Haystack' followed 'Shotgun' and 'Come See About Me' in the space of a few seconds. The movement of his jaw worked in time with the primitive flashing lights, as he folded a new stick of Wrigleys and pushed it between his teeth. Then 'Not Fade Away' caused the lights to flash more rapidly and his jaw involuntarily kept pace, so that he could no longer feel his teeth and had to prod his mouth to make sure they were still there.

The movement on the dancefloor became a blur of patterns and lights and the electricity in his head fizzed and buzzed, with the music powering the current.

"Are you not talking tonight?" The voice was distant, as if echoing down a long corridor and he only realised it was real when he felt a tug on the sleeve of his jacket and turned to see Christine, her eyes flashing white against thick, black kohl circles.

"Sorry, just watching everyone."

"I know, I've been waving to you for the last ten minutes. You were dancing like you were in a trance." She smiled and took his hand, pulling him towards the dancefloor.

The Righteous Brothers slowed the pace and as Christine's hand touched his shirt, Alan realised he was soaked in sweat, his jaw ached and thoughts flashed through his mind like a film reel played at double speed. He reached into his top pocket and retrieved a small brown envelope, tipping the contents into his mouth. Catching Christine's eye, he sensed a glint of excitement.

"You want one?"

"Are they teardrops?"

Alan nodded and Christine closed her eyes and pushed out her tongue, onto which he dropped a half-pill.

"My mum's staying at her sister's tonight." Christine looked back over her shoulder as she span away, the trumpet intro of '1-2-3' cutting clumsily across the final chords of 'You've Lost that Loving Feeling'.

"So you can stay out later?" Alan pulled her close and shouted in her ear.

"Well yes, but..." She smiled and tilted her head and Alan wondered what it meant.

"It means you don't have to go home when you drop me off."

He was no good at reading the signs, never had been, and he felt the knot tighten in his stomach as Christine shook her head and laughed, catching her friend's eye across the dancefloor. Elaine looked over to him and waved, then leant in towards Wesley and whispered something in his ear and he laughed too. The room span, the lights flashed in sequence and the music burst from the speakers and exploded in his head. Alan shivered, suddenly chilled by the sweat soaked shirt sticking to his back. *Got a feeling inside, I can't explain.*

Chapter 29

Sunday 21 March 1965

The secanol had started to kick-in by the time Alan Connolly got off the number 8 bus opposite Watson Cairns, two milk-round kids in black PVC jackets with their noses to the window, coveting a '64 Plate Triumph Tiger, cash or HP for £199. He'd stopped shaking now but the light hurt his eyes and he was glad he'd been wearing his sunglasses despite yesterday's rain showers.

He stopped to rub a dancefloor stain from his white Sta-Prest trousers as he turned the corner from Lower Briggate into Boar Lane. A bus idled outside Alexandre Menswear and an old man pushed a wooden barrow filled with Saturday night rubbish, but apart from that the street was deserted. Leeds on a Sunday was like a different planet to the Saturday city.

He crossed the road, passing the Peel and the El Toro coffee bar, a single scooter parked outside. He peered through the steamed-up window, trying to see who it was. Probably a late all-nighter still blocked and unable to sleep, or someone, like him, whose girl had decided a cab was a better option than a scooter ride home in the rain.

He passed Jacomelli's and glanced up Upper Mill Hill towards La Conca d'Ora, the street deserted and cobbles still wet from the overnight downpours. Along Boar Lane past Thornton's Chocolate Kabin and the doorway leading up to Kee Hong Chinese Restaurant, the step spattered in beer-stink puke. Then turning right into Basinghall Street, stomach turning as he inhaled petrol and burnt rubber. Stepping over the hose pipes snaking from the back of the fire engine blocking the street opposite the Del Rio. Two oversized men in dark overalls and black helmets turned towards him, and he felt his heartbeat quicken and his chest tighten as he caught sight of the blackened skeleton of the Lambretta in the shadow of Mill Hill Chapel. *Fuck.Fuck.Fuck.*

"This yours son?" Another fireman was talking to Luigi outside the coffee bar.

"Yes, I left it last night." Alan's mouth felt dry and he squinted in the shock of daylight as he removed his sunglasses.

"Well you'll need to wait for the police to arrive. They'll want a statement."

"Police? Why what happened?" Alan felt his legs begin to shake and had to steel himself to remain upright. *Proper cunts. Use your head from now on.*

"Well, this was no accident. The petrol cap was off. Looks like someone stuffed a burning rag into it. Went up like a bomb, it was lucky no one was passing or they could have been killed."

"You want a drink of something? You don't look well." Gigi stepped forward and took hold of Alan's arm.

"No I'm okay...I just need to...I'll be back in a minute." Alan began to slowly back away down Basinghall Street. *Switch flicked. Electricity coursing through his brain, white lights flashing, blinding him.*

"The police will need to speak to you." The fireman stepped forward but Alan continued to back off, before turning and increasing his pace as he approached the corner, then jogging, stumbling, running along Boar Lane. Stopping to vomit on Kirkgate, then down past the

121

market, the abattoir, the smell of shit and death making him retch again. Then across the road to Quarry Hill flats. Through the blue entrance door, up the stairs- the lift usually works, but not today, chest heaving as he climbed the stairs, gasping for breath upon reaching the seventh floor. Along the walkway, looking down into the car park and up New York Street. No one following.

To his front door, key in hand, stopping in his tracks as he saw the words gouged into the blue paintwork.

'NOT MINE, NOT YOURS.'

Chapter 30

Strong arms around him. No escape.

Dark eyes smiling. Where's the monster.

Stubble kisses. Sweat and tobacco. Brylcream and beer.

Push him back. Brown eyes screaming.

Pencil in his neck. Blood on his hands.

Kill the monster. He's still alive.

Strong arms around him, slipping away.

Blue eyes crying. Who's the monster.

Police sirens. Sweat and tobacco. Blades and Buckfast.

Pull him back. Green eyes closed.

Knife in his chest. Blood on his hands.

Don't die Tam. He's already dead.

Chapter 31

Monday 22 March 1965

Pistol Fired in Leeds Street Melee– During a disturbance involving about 50 people in the centre of Leeds on Saturday night, a starting pistol was fired by a youth, it was alleged at Leeds City Court today. The disturbance, said Chief Inspector A.Beason, would appear to have had some connection to the Leeds United-Everton game played earlier in the day. Police officers were called to Vicar Lane at 10.10pm and found a group of around 50 young men who were involved in 'quite a melee.' As the officers arrived they heard a loud bang and an officer pursued Ronald Lockwood, 20, down Kirkgate, where he was arrested. Lockwood said later that he had bought the pistol for £2 "for a giggle and to frighten people".

"You look terrible old boy, when did you last sleep?" Stanley Mortimer screwed a cork bung into the top of a test tube and carefully placed it in a rack on the top shelf of a rusting fridge, then removed a surgical mask and turned to face Alan Connolly, while tightening the cord on his plaid dressing gown.

"I got a couple of hours this morning, but I keep having weird dreams. Once I wake up I can't go back to sleep, no matter how many downers I take." Alan perched on the settee, watching Sapphire sitting cross-legged in the corner of the room, eyes closed while muttering inaudible words, her hands jerking and twitching as she spoke.

"What's up with her?" Alan lowered his voice and nodded in the girl's direction.

"Don't worry about her. She's convinced her old shadow is trying to return. She's having a discussion with it at the moment." Stanley tapped at his temple and smiled and joined Alan on the couch.

"So the teardrops are selling well then?"

"Aye, people can't get enough of them and we need to step up the volume. There's a big Tamla Motown show at the Grand next week. There'll be kids there from all over Yorkshire. It's a great opportunity to expand the operation, get the product known."

"Well if you can provide the Drynamil, there's no problem with the acid. I've just cooked up a new mix, made it even more...interesting." Stanley tugged the dressing gown to cover his bare white knees as Sapphire slowly pulled herself upright in the corner, her eyes still closed.

"No problem. Now that we're only using half-pills I've got plenty left."

Both men fell silent as Sapphire began to emit a high pitched whine, her arms extended and her eyes cast towards the ceiling.

"Are you back with us my darling?" Stanley smirked as Sapphire slowly moved towards the centre of the room.

The whine became louder and deeper, and the girl's head began to sway from side to side, her matted hair falling over her face.

"Sapphire, we have a visitor. Your friend Alan has called to see us."

Her eyes open now, Sapphire put her hands to her face and began to wail as if afflicted by a sudden pain, sinking to her knees and rocking back and forth in front of the sofa.

"What's the matter with her?" Alan addressed Stanley in a hushed tone.

"Interesting isn't it? And quite dramatic. She gets worse than this. Á couple of days ago I had to tie her up to stop her jumping out of the window." Stanley giggled as he watched Sapphire begin to tear at the neck of her blouse, teeth bared and eyes wild.

"Why was she trying to jump out of the window?"

"She was convinced that a demon had led her old shadow back to her and that she needed to kill it again....come now, time to calm down, you're scaring our guest."

Stanley stood and walked into the kitchen, leaving Alan facing the writhing, snarling girl who had now pulled off her stained top and was staring with dark eyes that seemed to look straight through him.

"Mara is here, he's with us now." Sapphire's eyes opened wide but unseeing and a malevolent grin played upon her thin white lips as she crouched in front of Alan.

"Who's Mara?" Alan heard the fear in his own voice.

"Mara, God of death and his demon Namuci are here to obscure the knowledge of truth, to return my soul to its conditioned existence. Do you see...?" Sapphire whispered, her hushed voice filled with an urgency and her eyes darting from Alan towards the kitchen, and the sound of Stanley Mortimer filling a kettle.

"Tea old chap? It will do you good." Stanley's voice caused Sapphire to turn then crawl towards Alan.

"He is Mara! He is the shark swimming in the depths of my mind. He is trying to bring my shadow back to me. Do you see?" Sapphire bounded forward and placed her hands on Alan's thighs, her chemical breath causing him to recoil.

"Erm, Stanley...I think you need to do something." Alan instinctively raised his right hand to feel the comforting presence of the bayonet in the lining of his suit jacket as Sapphire positioned her face a couple of inches from his own.

"Me and you Alan...we're the same. Only we can see them."

Alan pushed himself back as far as the sofa would allow, and was glad to see Stanley hurry back into the room, flicking at a syringe. Sapphire flinched at his touch and jerked herself upright, looking up at him with eyes flashing angrily as he steadied her, brushing the hair from her face.

"Now then, got ourselves into a right old state again haven't we?"

Sapphire hissed through bared teeth and Alan felt a shiver run down his spine as Stanley placed his arm across her chest and pulled her back towards him.

"Time for your medicine...there we go." Stanley placed the syringe on her upper arm and depressed the plunger, his arm straining to hold her as she twisted in his grasp.

"There...sleep now." Stanley relaxed his grip as Sapphire sank backwards, her head resting on his chest, eyes closed, her words now a whisper.

"You and I...we're the same Alan...only we can see the demons."

Chapter 32

Tuesday 23 March 1965

Berlin: US Battalion Passes Through – Berlin, Saturday – The U.S. Army, in a demonstration of its access rights to Berlin, today sent a whole infantry battalion in battle order along the Berlin highway. The armed troops travelled along the 'auto bhan' route to Berlin in four convoys. The Russians passed the troops quickly and without difficulty through their Marienborn checkpoint on the East-West German border, 110 miles from Berlin. The Russians also ended their harassing flights in the Berlin air corridors as their recent military manoeuvres drew to a close.

"Get in." Father Ernest held open the door of the Rover saloon car and signalled towards the back seat with a flick of his black eyes.

Alan Connolly cast a glance upwards to the grey ramparts of Quarry Hill flats, ducked his head and climbed in, his eyes immediately stung by a pall of cigarette smoke.

Father Ernest gently closed the door and walked to the front of the car where he stood, hands behind his back, watching two small boys kicking a can against a wall.

"He said you wanted to see me..." Alan's question broke the silence but elicited no response, as Clive Donovan tilted his head to watch the fake priest observing the boys.

Alan rubbed at his sweat-soaked palms with his fingertips and listened to Donovan breathing beside him for several seconds.

"What games did you play as a child?" Donovan's voice was soft, almost a whisper, and his gaze remained on the two boys as he spoke.

"What? Me? Games...?" Alan was glad the silence had ended but was unsure how to respond or where the conversation was leading.

"Games. Play. Vital in the development of a child. They teach you social skills you see. Very important, especially for a boy." Donovan sucked on his cigarette and turned to breath the smoke into Alan's face.

"Aye, just normal stuff I guess. I didn't really have any toys..." *Brain wired wrong.*

"Were you beaten?" Clive Donovan emphasised the final word and licked at his cracked, bulbous lips.

Alan caught his breath and paused, hoping Donovan would continue, but he fell silent.

"My da' was strict enough, aye, so sometimes I suppose." Alan glanced sideways to see Donovan smiling gently, his eyes part-closed, head nodding gently.

  "Good." Donovan sighed and opened his eyes as Father Ernest turned to peer back into the car.

Alan stared out of the side window as the back seat fell silent again, so silent that he could hear his own heart beating in his chest, and he wondered if Donovan could hear it too as he fought the urge to get out of the car and run.

"Discipline is important." Donovan spoke eventually, stubbing his cigarette out in an ashtray in the door and immediately lighting another. "Especially for a boy like you. It's good that you were beaten. I'm pleased about that."

The silence descended again and Alan wasn't sure whether he should respond.

"Do you agree?" Donovan expelled a mouthful of smoke into Alan's face as he spoke.

"Aye, I suppose. It taught me a lesson I guess."

"A lesson. Yes. And what lesson did it teach you?" There was no pause this time, no silence.

"Erm, I suppose that if you do wrong, then you get punished?" Alan felt a movement on the seat beside him and prayed that Donovan's hand wasn't about to rest on his leg.

"Consequences. All actions have consequences. Yes. Good." Clive Donovan's hand settled on Alan's knee and he steeled himself to stop the leg shaking. Father Ernest rubbed at his chin as he stared into the car and licked at his top lip like a hungry cat.

"And I want you to bear that word, consequences, in mind over the coming days and weeks." Donovan's hand squeezed Alan's knee and he stared ahead through the windscreen and felt the sour, warm breath tickle his cheek.

"Do I make myself clear?"

"Erm...I think so, but why..?" Alan was mid-sentence when Donovan interjected, leaning in and whispering in his ear as his hand moved higher.

"The motorbike. I heard what happened, and you must trust me when I say that our mutual associate Mr. Cohen has suffered the consequences of his actions. There will not, and I repeat this to ensure you fully understand Alan, there will not be any further reprisals. The matter is closed. Do I make myself clear?" Alan could feel Donovan's lips touching his ear and his stare remained fixed on the front windscreen, beyond which Father Ernest glared back, a half-smile playing on his lips.

"Very clear." Alan's voice croaked his response and Clive Donovan gave his thigh a final squeeze.

"Good boy. Off you go then..."

Alan tugged at the door handle with a shaking hand and pushed it open with his knee, his eyes meeting Father Ernest's as he clambered out and hurried towards the entrance to the flats.

"Alan!"

He froze at the sound of Father Ernest's voice and turned to see the fake priest raise an index finger, his face solemn and beatific.

"Come in from the dark Alan. Renounce Satan and all his work and ways. Follow us. Follow us, for you are our son."

Alan swallowed hard and nodded and in the back seat of the Rover, Clive Donovan lit a cigarette and flashed a brown smile of decay and mouthed a silent word to him.

"Amen."

Chapter 33

Wednesday 24 March 1965

'Raid Link to Suspicious Death'. Leeds City Police today released the name of the employee whose body was discovered at the premises of West Leeds Printing Works on Saturday morning, following what they suspect to be a botched burglary.

The deceased man was 68 year old Horace Wilson of Aviary Mount, Armley. Mr. Wilson was a retired widower who had been employed at the works as a part-time night watchman for the last five years.

Detective Superintendent Godfrey Spring said that Mr. Wilson's body was discovered by workers arriving at the Armley works for their morning shift on Saturday, and subsequent investigations have revealed evidence of forced entry to an outbuilding, though it remains unclear what, if anything, was taken.

An autopsy carried out at Leeds General Infirmary yesterday has failed to provide a conclusive cause of death, but D.S. Spring made reference to a number of unexplained abrasions on Mr. Wilson's body and said that police are keeping an open mind on the incident whilst their enquiries continue.

Norman slowly lowered the Evening Post and looked first at Scotty, who covered his face with his hands, and then Wesley who blinked while chewing nervously.

"Whilst their enquiries continue...Shit, what does that mean?"

"It means they know fucking nothing, that's what it means." Alan stood in the kitchen doorway, his hands thrust deep into the front pockets of his Levi's.

"Unexplained abrasions though... That means they know he was roughed up." Scotty lowered his hands, his face grey.

"Unexplained means they don't know. We got rid of the washing line. There were no marks on his arms. He could have got the bruises and grazes doing his garden for all the police know."

"They don't have gardens in the Aviary's..." Norman's words tailed off as his eyes met Alan's.

"Just fucking shut up about it. The van hasn't been mentioned so they haven't linked it to this. All they have is a busted padlock on a warehouse full of waste paper and an old bloke who could have dropped dead at any time. They know nothing, believe me. It's good news, so stop worrying." Alan turned and walked into the kitchen and pushed at the ignition button on the gas stove. *Spark igniting the gas. Spark in his brain turning on the electricity.*

"Good news that we killed someone." Wesley muttered under his breath.

"What was that Wesley? You got something to say?" Alan's voice from the kitchen caused the three youths to look at each other, then down at their own shuffling feet.

"Fucking hell lads, how have we got ourselves into this?" Wesley, whispering now, got no reaction from his friends as he picked up the paper and looked down at the plump face, the medals on the smart suit jacket, the neatly combed hair and the smiling eyes that stared back at him from the page. 'Horace Wilson,68, night watchman'. Wesley ran his finger along the caption before putting his thumb over the face in the picture.

"We killed him, and apparently that's good news. What the fuck have we turned into lads?"

Chapter 34

Friday 26 March 1965

Beat Music Led to Beat-Ups – A licensee told Harrogate magistrates that 'beat' music sessions had attracted troublemakers, so it changed its dances to rhythm and blues. Mr Lloyd Griffiths of the Adelphi Hotel said that since the change in tempo, dances had been perfectly orderly. He was responding to the comments of Insp. Stanley Armitage who said that police had been called to disturbances at dances on numerous occasions and opposed an application for a block of licence extensions for Saturday all-night dance events.

The fact that the disc jockey had purchased half a dozen teardrops from Alan as soon as he'd entered the BG club was becoming evident by 2am. 'Fingertips' by Little Stevie Wonder pulsed from the speakers for the third time in twenty minutes and the packed dancefloor seemed to move as one, the uplifting harmonica solo saluted by a sea of raised arms. The young man operating the turntable moved in time to the music, eyes closed and his grinning face cast towards the ceiling.

Alan discarded his gum into an empty coke bottle and watched Scotty and Norman spinning and reeling around two girls dressed in identical white plastic rain macs, dancing close together whilst pretending to ignore the attentions of the two youths. Alan unwrapped another stick of Wrigley's and folded it into his mouth, then shivered as his friends' grinning, sweat soaked faces were illuminated in the flashing red light, taking on a suddenly malevolent appearance. Alan closed his eyes to dispel images of a blood soaked satanic ritual which now flooded his brain. *Only we can see the demons.*

A nudge in the small of his back caused him to turn to see Christine. Dressed in a maroon M+S twinset and knee-high leather boots, she smiled then took his hand and pulled him towards her. Over Christine's shoulder, Alan nodded to acknowledge Elaine and Wesley who were standing by the bar. Elaine responded with a theatrically blown kiss, while Wesley quickly turned away.

"Come and dance." 'Baby Love' was blasting from the speakers and the DJ had left his position on the turntables and was now in the midst of the dancers. Christine's eyes flashed bright, brilliant white with pinprick pupils, surrounded by thick, black kohl rings, and Alan followed her onto the dancefloor, avoiding the attentions of Scotty and Norman who left the girls and bounced towards them, heads nodding in time to the music. *All you do is treat me bad.*

Red, purple, green. The sequence of the flashing lights coupled with the music seemed hypnotic and time seemed to lose meaning. Sometimes it felt that the same song had been playing for hours, then another was ended before Alan remembered it even beginning. Checking his watch, the big hand hadn't moved since the last time he'd looked. A few minutes later he checked it again and the small hand had shifted by an hour. His jaw ached from constant chewing and his calf muscles felt like they were about to explode, but he'd never felt so full of energy, ambition and ideas in his life. *Nothing gets in my way, not even locked doors.*

Then a sudden wave of crippling fatigue hit him, and the sticky dance floor seemed to have locked his heavy feet in position. That lasted only until he reached into his jacket pocket and produced another pill. His mood shifted with every song and the sequence of the flashing lights seemed to trip him from confidence into self-doubt, from sadness to euphoria, calmness to agitation. Red.Green.Purple. Slowly, the realisation dawned that the disc jockey was using the lights and the music to hypnotise him. *Only we can see the demons.*

Alan looked across towards the young man on the small stage who was now flicking through a case of records, obviously trying to select the next tune which would determine his mood. He reached into the lining of his jacket and felt his breath quicken as he caressed the cold, hard steel of the bayonet while staring at the DJ. *Wired wrong. Electricity crackling and buzzing. Voices too loud to ignore.*

 Christine danced between Alan and the DJ stand, her eyes fixed on his, unable to detect the danger they were both in, smiling, singing along to the Miracles, as Alan glanced left to see Norman, Scotty and Wesley talking, their heads close together, plotting, scheming. *Only we can see them.*

The lights flashed red as Norman tossed back his head, his mouth wide, teeth flashing red and purple, and Alan watched as Wesley caught the DJ's green eyes, sending him signals, what to play, which of Alan's emotions should be switched on and off. He reached into his jacket and gripped the hilt of the bayonet. Before he was able to withdraw it, the flashing red and purple and green turned black and a pair of warm, moist hands covered his eyes.

Struggling free, Alan turned and immediately felt wet lips on his, a face too close, dark hair concealing its features.

"Hey baby." Sapphire draped her arms around his neck and pushed her crotch against his thigh, thrusting it in time to the music. Stanley Mortimer looked on from the edge of the dancefloor, smirking and raising two coke bottles in greeting.

"We've been to the Three Coins to see the Outer Limits. It was groovy! Stanley wanted to come and see if everyone is digging his trip...looks like they are!" She laughed and threw back her head, spinning away while keeping hold of Alan's hand.

He tried to pull loose and turned to see Christine, no longer smiling, no longer singing along to the music. Her arms folded, she looked from Alan to Sapphire then back to Alan, her eyes seeking an answer.

"That's Sapphire, she's Stanley's girlfriend. I told you about him." Alan leant forward to shout his explanation into her ear, but she was already turning away, heading across the dancefloor towards Elaine.

"Chrissy!" Alan began to follow her but was halted by a skeletal bare arm reaching across his chest.

"Come and dance with me Alan. Don't you want me?" Sapphire wiggled her hips and ran her hands down from her breasts across her stomach and on to her crotch, leaving them there, slowly caressing herself and causing dancing couples to move away, heads shaking.

"No. I can't..." Alan felt the sweat-soaked walls begin to close in, the flashing lights illuminating the faces of the other dancers, transforming them into living waxworks.

He watched as Christine cupped her hand and spoke into Elaine's ear, her friend looking over, lips pursed in distaste as she watched Sapphire writhing behind him.

"You need to go..." Alan took hold of Sapphire's shoulders and attempted to push her towards Stanley Mortimer who seemed to be enjoying the show, laughing on the edge of the dancefloor, tapping the coke bottles together in time to the music.

"Go?! I'm not going anywhere baby. Stanley chased the shadow away again, tonight is my night!" Sapphire wriggled free and wrapped her arms around Alan's neck, then vaulted forward, wrapping her legs around his waist, her tongue lapping at his mouth.

"Sapphire, I'm not joking, get the fuck off me..." Alan gripped her arms, struggling to break free. He leant forward, prising her arms from him and deposited her onto the coke-soaked floor. She lay on her back on the sticky surface, laughing hysterically, arms and legs flailing wildly. Alan turned to see that the dancefloor had cleared and the red and green and purple faces were all staring at him. Norman and Scotty seemed to be suppressing smiles and Wesley leant in and whispered something to Elaine. Christine's face crumpled and she stepped forward, streaks of kohl stark against the white of her cheeks.

"I'm going home now."

"No Chrissy, don't go. She's pissed and blocked that's all. She's with her boyfriend, she's nothing to do with me." Alan tried to take hold of her hand but Christine backed away, then looked past him as Sapphire hauled herself from the dancefloor and swayed up to them as 'Where did our Love Go' began to play.

"Is this your little sister Alan...or your mother?" Sapphire looked down at Christine's outfit and shook her head.

"At least I'm not a state like you!" Christine stepped forward, her fists clenched and Alan raised a hand in front of her chest.

"Aw, Grandma getting angry?" Sapphire sneered, moving alongside Alan and putting her arm around his waist. "You need to take a look at your wardrobe and make-up honey, a new look might stop your boy getting his kicks elsewhere."

"You lying bitch! She's lying Alan, isn't she?" Christine's tears began to flow as Alan struggled to release himself from Sapphire's grip.

"Lying huh? I could prove it by telling you about his birthmark, but I doubt you've ever had your head that close to his dick...am I right?"

Sapphire erupted in laughter as Christine turned and dashed across the dancefloor towards the door, closely followed by Elaine and Wesley.

"Why the fuck did you do that?" Alan shook his head as Sapphire cackled with delight and twirled her flowing skirt as she danced before him.

"I freed you, that's what I did." She leant in, raising her voice to be heard over the music. "You say you don't want to turn into your father? So don't marry the same girl he did. A normal girl, school, job, marriage, house, babies, middle age, death. You're different Alan, you're like us. You can leave that shadow behind. Now is your time to be free. Come with me, let me teach you how to fly."

Sapphire shook her head and turned away, swaying across the dancefloor towards Stanley Mortimer who clapped and smiled and indulged her like a father watching a toddler at play.

Alan stood alone in the centre of the dancefloor and closed his eyes, letting the music wash over him, sensing the changing colour of the lights, red, green, purple, feeling the stares of the others, hearing their laughter, struggling to contain his rage. *Black electricity fizzing in his brain, lightning flashing and burning, voices too loud to ignore.*

His heart pounded hard in his chest and he struggled to control his breathing, but kept his eyes closed tight, until he sensed Sapphire dancing in front of him, smelling her sweat, her breath on his ear. *See the demons.*

"Lose that shadow Alan, come learn to fly with me...or stick with this life, turn into your father and die here."

Chapter 35

Screaming. Shouting. Hands on his neck.

Water filling his mouth. Water filling his nose.

Screaming. Shouting. Hands on his neck. Hands on his head.

Water in his mouth. Water in his nose. Tears in his eyes.

Hands on his neck, hands round his throat.

You're killing the boy.

Why do you make me do it.

Screaming. Shouting. Hands on his hands.

Water in his mouth. Water in his nose. Tears in his eyes.

Don't kill the boy.

Hands on his hands. Arms round his neck.

Why do you make me. Tears in their eyes.

Water in his mouth, water in his nose, water on the tiles.

Tears in their eyes. Blue eyes crying.

Red, purple, green.

You've killed the boy.

Chapter 36

Saturday 27 March 1965

April 5 is Meter Day - The 1230 new parking 'meters'
will click into action in the centre of Leeds along with
the second stage of the one-way traffic system on
Monday April 5, it has been announced. Thirty six meter
attendants will be employed by Leeds Corporation to
enforce the new parking meter regulations. They are
likely to be seen some days before April 5 familiarising
themselves with their beats. Cost of installing the meters
is put at about £45,000 and an income of £65,000 is
expected from them in the financial year 1965-66. Any
profit will be used to provide off-street car parking
places in the city centre.

"Leeds.. Leeds.. Leeds.. Leeds." The slow, rhythmic chant
began in the top corner of the Hillsborough Kop's huge
sloping open terrace, and increased in volume as it was
picked up by those below, eventually being countered by
a response of 'United, United', from the Manchester
supporters.

The old stadium was full to its 65,000 capacity for the
cup semi-final but the wide terrace steps felt less packed
and were missing the crowd surges that Alan, Wesley,
Norman and Scotty were used to in the corner of the
Scratching Shed. They'd secured a position to the left of
the goal, parallel with the cross bar and Alan grimaced as
the child behind them, perched on a barrier, span his
rattle again, the ear-splitting noise inches from his head.

"I'm going to take that off the wee shite in a minute," he
grumbled, but none of his friends were listening.

The first half had begun with Leeds looking lively, prompted by skipper Bobby Collins in midfield, they poured forward with Man. Utd saved on a couple of occasions by goalkeeper Pat Dunne. The reds successfully soaked up the early pressure, with eleven men behind the ball at times. They also looked dangerous on the break, with wingers Best and Connelly causing problems for the Leeds defence.

Leeds had a strong wind at their backs and Don Revie's game plan soon became apparent as high balls were thrown forward, aiming for the head of striker Alan Peacock, but the Yorkshire fans started to become frustrated as repeated attacks broke down and the game became scrappy and bad tempered.

The second half began in a similar vein as Nobby Stiles flattened Jim Storrie, Bremner felled Best and Leeds were temporarily reduced to ten men when Johanneson limped off following a tackle by Crerand. The feeling that referee Whittle was losing control of the game was confirmed as a melee developed into a full-blown brawl involving Bremner and Charlton, Law and Crerand.

"Go on Billy, knock him out!" For Alan, the prospect of a fist fight, especially one involving some good Scottish boys, was the highlight of the afternoon.

With order restored, Leeds weathered a brief Man. Utd storm as Bobby Charlton picked up a miscued clearance from his brother Jack, took aim and pulled the trigger. The ball was deflected for a corner which Leeds defended with all ten outfield players in the box.

"One goal is going to win this," Scotty speculated.

"Neither team wants to win it enough though. They're both scared of losing it now, with ten minutes to go."

Wesley shook his head as Stiles was booked for a shoulder charge which took out a flying Johanneson.

"Replay's at Nottingham on Wednesday if it stays 0-0. There's a special leaving at half two. I fancy that rather than 'bus..." Wesley shouted back towards his friends but was cut short by Alan.

"What...this coming Wednesday?"

"Yeah, they've already said it's at 'City Ground. It's 14/6 on 'train. Only a couple more shillings than with Heaps or Wally Arnold, so we might as well..."

"We can't go." Alan's words were lost as the crowd roared in response to a Connelly cross which flew into the Leeds goal mouth to be cleared by Jack Charlton.

"What did you say?" Wesley was stood on the step below Alan and half turned and shouted behind him, while maintaining his focus on the pitch.

"I said we can't go. It's the Motown show at the Odeon on Wednesday. We all need to be there to do the pills. It's a big opportunity." Alan waited for a response but none came. Scotty and Norman shuffled nervously on the terrace step but Wesley continued to stare straight ahead without speaking.

"There's a few scores to be settled out there on Wednesday," observed a ruddy faced man wearing a Leeds rosette on his donkey jacket, as the referee raised his whistle and signalled an end to the bad tempered goalless draw.

"I'm sorry boys, but business is business..." Alan faced his friends as they turned to begin their slow exit from the terrace.

Scotty and Norman nodded and exchanged fleeting glances but remained silent.

Wesley narrowed his eyes and straightened the hood of his parka, then ascended the terrace step, brushing past Alan who stepped aside to let him past. The boy on the barrier was being helped down by his father and saluted the departing players with a final twist of his wooden rattle. The sound coincided with Wesley's muttered words, which Alan, Norman and Scotty all pretended not to hear.

"You can fuck off Alan if you think I'm missing 'game on Wednesday. I'm off to Nottingham whether you like it or not."

Chapter 37

Monday 29 March 1965

US Helicopters Lost in Vietnam – Saigon, Saturday – Three American helicopters were reported shot down by Communist Viet-Cong ground fire today. They were airlifting troops into an area thick with guerillas about 350 miles north-east of Saigon. U.S Military sources said at least two American pilots were killed. Twenty other helicopters taking part in the operation were also hit by fire from an unknown number of Viet-Cong on the ground. There may be more American casualties.

"I hope we didn't disturb you Alan. Not got a young lady in there have you?" Clive Donovan nodded towards the bedroom and Father Ernest left the room with a disdainful curl of his lip and a glance in Alan's direction.

"No, I live on my own." Alan rubbed at his eyes and straightened his hair, exchanging glances with his brother who was perched on the edge of the settee, biting his lower lip and exposing his missing front teeth.

"Hmmm...because I heard you'd got yourself a young lady friend." Donovan smirked as Father Ernest re-entered the room shaking his head.

Alan sat down alongside his brother and felt Donovan's gaze settle upon his greying Y-fronts.

"No, we fell out."

"Ahh...Hands that never touch. Lips that never meet. Almost lovers, never to be.... The course of young love rarely runs smoothly Alan."

Donovan reached into his jacket pocket and retrieved a silver case, from which he extracted a thin cigarette between thumb and index finger.

"I trust that any negative repercussions relating to your failed affairs of the heart haven't impinged on your ability to conduct business?" Donovan tickled the tip of the cigarette with a lighter flame and sent a cloud of smoke drifting into a shaft of sunlight which escaped through a gap in the curtains.

"Sorry...what?" Alan's voice croaked a response. He'd been roused by the 8am knock on the flat door, to be greeted by Keith, eyes flickering with concern, closely followed by Donovan and Father Ernest, and his voice still felt hoarse from Saturday afternoon on the Hillsborough terraces.

"He means keep your mind on business..." Father Ernest spoke quietly and Alan felt his brother flinch at the looming presence standing behind them.

"....and not on sin." The chemical smell of mothballs and old tobacco registered first on Alan's senses as the dark sleeve of the priest's leather trench coat brushed his shoulder, leaning across him from behind the settee. The hand, with its bluebird tattoo between thumb and index finger seemed to pause for a long second in front of his eyes, before resuming its descent.

Alan took a deep breath and closed his eyes as Father Ernest's hand gripped his testicles and squeezed hard.

"Keep this in your pants and focus on the job." Clive Donovan's eyes flashed with excitement as Alan tried to stifle a cry.

"I will...I am." Alan exhaled loudly as Father Ernest released his grip and walked to the window, pulling on a pair of black leather gloves.

"That's what you say Alan, but sales are down. You've not needed a resupply after the weekend, still got pills left over from last week. That's never happened before."

"It's been quiet in town with the weather being bad, less kids are buying pills, but the security takings are up, everyone paying on time..."

"Your saving grace!" Donovan stood up and exhaled a cloud of smoke which descended slowly towards the settee, causing Alan to blink.

"The security income is good, excellent in fact. And that's the reason I'm prepared to give you a chance to improve your performance on the pills. If it wasn't for that, your employment would have been...terminated." Donovan dropped his cigarette on the carpet and stubbed it out with his foot.

"You'll sort it out, and quickly Alan, or we'll need a further discussion on the matter." He signalled towards the flat door with a tilt of his head and Father Ernest slowly rubbed his gloved hands together while staring at Alan, stooping to whisper to Keith as he left.

"Fix it. You brought him in, if he becomes a problem, it's your problem."

The brothers sat in silence looking at their feet until they heard the latch click on the front door and Keith stood and peered nervously into the empty hallway.

"Have they gone?" Alan stood up but was immediately knocked backwards onto the couch as his brother stormed back into the room.

"What the fuck Alan? What are you up to?"

"What? What have I done?" Alan raised his arms to protect himself as his brother lunged forward, fists clenched.

"You fucking stupid...stupid little bastard!" Alan pushed himself off the settee and shuffled backwards until he could go no further and pressed his back against the wall, standing to face his brother.

"You tell me what's going on Alan, tell me the truth, now! None of this bullshit about no one buying pills because of the weather..." Keith's chest heaved and the veins in his neck pulsed and Alan recognised that rage, the hair-trigger temper they'd all inherited from their father. *Wired wrong.*

"Honestly Keith, I'm not lying."

"Fucking hell Alan!" Keith launched himself forward and grabbed Alan by the throat then drove his forehead hard into his brother's face, sending Alan spinning back, his head hitting the wall.

"Stop fucking lying to me, stop lying, stop fucking lying!" A flurry of punches landed on the back of Alan's head as he slumped forward and he glimpsed his suit jacket hanging on the back of a chair, the bayonet in the lining causing it to sag down to the right.

Kicks now in his abdomen, stamps on his ribs and Alan looked at the jacket with the bayonet, the bayonet which in any other situation, with any other person, would now be in his hand, plunged into the guts of his assailant as he took control of the situation, turning the tables, saving himself.

"Fucking liar Alan, you're a fucking liar!"

Alan curled in a ball on the floor, felt the force of the assault begin to ebb as his brother's fury gave way to quiet sobs.

"Fucking liar... Stop... Fucking... Lying. Liar."

Alan removed his hands from the back of his head and exhaled blood from his nostrils as he slowly raised himself onto his knees. Keith was sat on the settee, his head in his hands, rocking back and forth.

"Just tell me the truth Alan. I'm your brother for fucks sake, I don't want to hurt you. I want to help you!"

Alan wiped at the blood dripping from his nose with the back of his hand and grimaced as he pulled himself upright.

"Okay, I was lying about less kids buying pills, I'm sorry."

"Jesus Alan, you can't do stuff like that with Donovan. He's not stupid. They have bouncers at most of the clubs working for them, they know what's going on. You'll get us both fucking killed."

Alan rubbed at a large bump which was forming on the back of his head.

"I know, but I was scared. I fucked it up."

"Why? What have you done? Why are there loads of pills left over from last week's supply?"

Alan swallowed hard and walked towards the window, looking out towards the bus station, two-tone green double deckers negotiating the pot holes and puddles.

Tell the truth. He's your brother. Just two wee Scottish boys against the world.

"I fucked it up. Stopped concentrating. Let the lads get sidetracked by the football and stuff. Because of Chrissy." *Fucking liar.*

"The lassie you were seeing?"

"Aye, I think us splitting up has bothered me more than I thought. Knocked my confidence a bit." *Stop fucking lying.*

"For fuck's sake man. Why didn't you tell me? That's what big brothers are for you stupid wee cunt..."

"Too proud I guess. But don't worry. I'll get things back on track. I know I've got to get my head straight again."

Keith stood and walked towards the window, reaching out to place his hands on Alan's shoulders.

"Shite, I've busted your nose up good there. I'm sorry brother."

"Reckon I probably deserved it..."

"Aye, maybe. Promise me you're okay now though. That you'll get things back on track?"

"Don't worry, I'll sort it out." Alan turned to look out of the window.

"You need to brother. Because make no mistake, we're in big trouble if you don't. Both of us. More trouble than we've ever known."

Chapter 38

Wednesday 31 March 1965

Sterling Talks in Paris 'Friendly' – Prime Minister Harold Wilson said today that his talks here with General de Gaulle had been remarkably friendly. He told a press conference attended by about 300 French and foreign journalists - 'In manner they have been courteous. In substance they have been outspoken, robust and constructive.' It was reported in the British camp earlier that the French president had been sympathetic to problems concerning the stability of the pound and might use his influence to ease pressure to devalue the currency from hostile French financiers.

"How did it go at the Wimpy Scotty?" Alan leant on a railing outside the Flamenco Coffee Bar on Cross Belgrave Street as he watched his friend crossing the road in front of the Wrens pub.

"Sold ten. Mostly just schoolkids in there for 'early show. Hopefully 'half eight one will be busier."

"Fuck." Alan looked at his watch. "We need a massive night tonight. Have to sell all the halves from last week as well as this week's supply."

"Can't we ditch 'teardops and go back to selling full pills?" Scotty removed his hands from his parka pockets to straighten his tie.

"We can't go back now, we have to stick to the plan. No one wants normal blues anymore after what we've been selling. This is our big chance. No going back." *A man with no plan ends up back where he started.*

"I can't believe it. Supremes, Martha and the Vandellas, Little Stevie, Smokey Robinson and even after they added Georgie Fame to the bill, ticket sales have still been shit." Norman kicked a Rothmans King Size packet into the gutter.

"They shouldn't have put two shows on. What's point of one at half six? Young kids want fucking 'Beatles not Motown." Scotty looked down the road as a gaggle of late arriving teenagers jogged towards the Odeon.

"And where the fuck is Wesley?" Alans question didn't require an answer. Not seen since the weekend, it confirmed what they all knew -that he didn't intend to miss the semi-final replay.

"Fucking wanker." Alan spat his gum into the gutter as Scotty and Norman nervously shifted their feet and stared down Upper Briggate, then retrieved two pills from the pocket of his parka and fed them into his mouth, followed by a new stick of gum.

"Wanker." Under his breath as he resumed his relentless chewing while looking down at the railing, watching his knuckles turning white.

Norman checked his watch and tried to change the subject. "Come on, let's go get a burger before we go to 'show. Back to 'Wimpy?"

"No. Carousel. More chance of shifting some pills there." Alan nodded towards two scooters parked on the pavement outside the café.

"You're a hard taskmaster boss. We don't even get a lunch break!" Scotty smiled, but his comment failed to lighten the mood as Alan pushed his hands deep into the pockets of his parka and stepped forward, glancing left down North Street, seeing the grey sky turning black above the mock Tudor shop fronts.

"I'm running out of time Scotty. We need a big night...a big week. Otherwise...there is no otherwise. We need to shift all these pills. Failure isn't an option."

Chapter 39

Friday April 2, 1965

United Conquering Heroes are Home -The triumphant Leeds United team arrived back in Leeds from their Grantham HQ yesterday afternoon and about 100 people were at Central station to greet them. When their train pulled in, Leeds United manager Don Revie, captain Bobby Collins and the goal scoring hero Billy Bremner were surrounded by back-slapping, hand shaking fans. In Nottingham, railway police were continuing enquiries into an after match incident in which stones shattered two windows of a Leeds bound train. As a football special left an adjoining platform for Manchester, supporters shouting "get back to Leeds" threw stones at the Leeds train. A 16 year old Manchester United supporter is to appear in court in connection with an alleged attack on match referee Mr. Dick Windle, police said today.

"Two games in three days again, I'm starting to think that Wesley is right and it's a conspiracy to stop us winning 'double." Scotty tapped his Pepsi bottle on the formica topped table in the Del Rio coffee bar.

"West Ham tomorrow shouldn't be a problem, they've got their eye on 'Cup Winners cup. Stoke on Monday will be tricky though." Norman shouted his response without turning from the pinball table where Non-stop Nigel was muttering inaudibly at the tilt light flashing intermittently in his eyeline.

"Chelsea will beat Birmingham but Blackburn have a good chance at home against Man. Utd." Scotty ran his fingers down the fixtures listed in the Evening Post. "And still no news on cup final tickets."

"Where is he anyway?" Alan had been staring silently at an overflowing ashtray, his chin buried deep in the collar of his parka.

Scotty cast a glance towards Norman, who maintained his focus on the silver ball which was bouncing between two buffers at the top of the table.

"Who?"

"You fucking know who...Wes."

"Not seen him, but I know he was doing his rounds yesterday. The florist in 'market gave me some cash to give him."

Alan didn't respond, his gaze remaining fixed on the ashtray, and the silence was broken only by the hiss of the coffee machine and the buzzes and chimes of the pinball table, until the distant rattle of a scooter engine prompted Norman to look towards the door as it opened, then quickly turn away again.

"Alright lads." Wesley pulled a chair from beneath the table and removed a Leeds scarf then began to unbutton his parka.

"Now then," Scotty glanced upwards momentarily and shuffled in his seat. Alan's gaze didn't shift from the ashtray as Wesley draped his parka over a seat back and shouted towards the counter for a coffee.

"You going tomorrow?" Wesley pulled another seat from beneath the table and sat down. "We'll need to get there early I reckon, should be a big crowd."

"Yeah, course." Scotty nodded as Alan retrieved a teaspoon from the sugar bowl and began to tap it on an empty cup on the table in front of him.

The obvious, unasked question was contributing to the tension and after a long minute, Norman turned away from the pinball machine. "Take it you went then?"

Alan slowly raised his eyes from the ashtray and stared at Wesley as he answered.

"Yeah, it was ace. Have you seen Billy's goal on Television?"

Norman shook his head as Wesley avoided eye contact with Alan. "No, a backwards header wasn't it? Read about it in 'paper."

"I got on 'pitch at 'end. It were great! I shook Bobby Collins' hand."

"What about Wembley? Has Elaine heard owt about tickets?" Scotty picked at his fingernails, feeling the weight of Alan's stare across the table.

"Yeah, they'll be announcing it tomorrow. We've only got 15,000. They go on sale to season ticket holders on April 18th then to anyone with 24 tokens the day after."

"How many season ticket holders are there?"

"Just short of five thousand. It's not going to be easy getting a ticket. They're controlling it a lot more now, so Elaine's got no chance of putting any aside."

Norman opened his mouth to speak but no words followed, as he thought better of making any reference to tokens.

"Thanks Luigi." Wesley pushed a sauce bottle aside to make room for the coffee cup that was placed before him, and Norman turned back towards the pinball machine. Scotty focused on the sugar bowl and picked harder at his fingernails as Alan tapped the teaspoon on the saucer while staring hard at Wesley. *Clink.Clink.Clink.*

"Go on then, say it." Wesley took a sip from his coffee, then lowered the cup, making eye contact with Alan for the first time.

Alan's face remained impassive, unblinking, as if he was looking straight through Wesley. *Switch flicked. Current flowing. Voices whispering, getting louder.*

"Say it..." A vein in Wesley's temple twitched and his fingers tapped on his thighs beneath the table.

The hint of a smile played on Alan Connolly's lips but his eyes betrayed no emotion. *Clink.Clink.Clink. Voices louder.*

"I've followed United since I was a kid. Saw King John score 39 in 41 games in '56. Home and away for 'last four years. Since before Revie, when we were at 'bottom of 'second division. Now we're one step from Wembley and going for 'league title too. There was no way...no way I could miss that game."

"Go on Nige...oooh yes!" Norman attempted to distance himself from the conversation as the pinball table rattled and buzzed, and Scotty directed his gaze towards the back of Nigel's sheepskin rather than at the table in front of him.

"So I missed 'Motown show, but I was back working 'next morning. I collected from 'tobacconist at 'bus station when they opened at half seven, you can ask them."

"It doesn't matter." Alan's voice was low and calm, as if speaking to himself and his unexpected response caused Wesley to pause.

"It was 'biggest game of our lifetimes, some things are more important than work. If you can call what we do work."

"What's that supposed to mean?" Alan continued to stare at the teaspoon in his hand, gently tapping the saucer. *Dark current fizzing below the surface. Under control. For now. Clink.Clink.Clink.*

Scotty caught Wesley's eye and gently shook his head.

"Nowt...How'd it go anyway, 'Motown night?"

Scotty grimaced and flinched, telling Wesley with his eyes not to go there.

"Shite. You didn't miss owt." Norman making it worse without turning from the pinball table.

"Not good, we hardly shifted owt. It were half empty, I think only the London gigs have sold out." Scotty tried to close the subject down before it escalated. *Clink.Clink.Clink.*

"Alright, enough about Wednesday, what's done is done. Come on, busy night ahead lads."

Alan pushed the chair back and replaced the teaspoon in the bowl, fastening the top button of his suit jacket as he stood up and nodded towards the door.

"I'll make 'time up Alan. I'll stay at 'Coins all-nighter till 'end tonight." Wesley looked up as Alan put on his parka and retrieved a handful of change from his pocket.

Alan Connolly placed the coins on the table and brushed past Wesley, then paused and leant forward to whisper in his ear.

"Last chance Wesley. You're either working with us or you're not. With us or against us. Decision time." *Tick Tock.*

Chapter 40

Screaming. Shouting. Hands on his neck. Hands on his head.

Water filling his mouth. Water filling his nose. Water filling his eyes.

You're killing the boy. Why do you make me do it.

Tears in his eyes. Blue eyes crying. Blue eyes dying.

Hands on his neck. Hands round his throat.

You're killing the boy. Screaming. Shouting.

Water in his mouth. Water in his nose. Tears in his eyes.

Cold white tiles. Water on the tiles.

Cold red tiles. Blood on the tiles.

Tears in his eyes. Blue eyes crying.

Tears in their eyes.

Brown eyes crying. Green eyes crying.

Blue eyes dying.

Chapter 41

Saturday, 3 April 1965

*Moon Pictures Support Landing Hopes- Pasadena
(California) -Photographs taken by the Ranger-9 craft
indicate that the moon's surface may be solid enough to
support a landing vehicle, making manned flight
possible, Dr Gerard Kuiper of the University of Arizona
said today. He dispelled some of the doubt about
whether the moon's surface might crumble under the
weight of a space vehicle and said, at a guess that it
looked as though it would be sufficient to support a ton
or two of weight per square foot.*

"Bet Wesley's still in bed if he stopped at 'Coins till it
closed." Scotty jogged to catch up with Alan and Norman
as they pushed against the flow of the fast moving crowds
heading up Lowfields Road from the specials bus stand
behind the Popular side.

"Keeping out of my way more likely." Alan paused
alongside Norman as he handed over sixpence to a
programme vendor on the corner of Elland Road
opposite the recently rebuilt Old Peacock pub. "Still two
hours to kick off, are we having a pint?"

"No, let's get in. They reckon there'll be over forty
thousand here today...oh fuck, look at the queue."

A five-deep line filling the pavement and spilling out
onto the road stretched along the entire length of the
Scratching Shed.

"Shall we try 'Kop? Weather's looking okay so we
shouldn't get wet." Scotty paused but Norman carried on
walking.

"No, we'll be alright. Looks like all 'turnstiles are open so we'll be in before two. Better atmosphere in 'shed."

"You two get in the queue, I'm off for a burger." Alan dodged a pile of fresh horse shit and jogged across Elland Road towards a Westler's stand outside the petrol station.

The vendor was a horse-faced teenager wearing a stained, white plastic jacket. His hare lip caused a slurring of the letter S, which resulted in Alan being sprayed with saliva when asked if he wanted onions with his burger.

The youth's lank, side-parted fringe flopped over one eye as he stooped to prod a rusting fork into the bubbling yellow liquid, and retrieve a grey patty which steamed and stank as he thrust it into a sliced breadcake and handed it to Alan.

Alan surveyed the scene as he took a bite of the burger. He'd always thrived on the energy of a football crowd. The tension and nervous anticipation seemed a natural extension of the adrenaline current which sparked sporadically in his own brain. That energy seemed amplified now as the season entered its final stages and the Leeds fans enjoyed the unfamiliar sensation of chasing glory on two fronts.

Alan watched as the fans teemed across Elland Road, jogging, fast-walking, dodging through the crowds, all eager to ensure their entry to the ground before the gates closed. Fathers carrying milk crates dragged sons in LUFC bobble hats towards the Popular Side; teenage girls in overlong scarves embroidered with the names of the team swigged from coke bottles; youths in suit jackets and sheepskins and white scarves with blue and yellow stripes hurried towards the kop; a skittish police horse danced onto the pavement, scattering fans in its wake.

He stuffed the final handful of stale bap and congealed, unidentifiable protein into his mouth and headed back across the road, drinking in the smells of Bovril and ale, tobacco and sweat. Scotty spotted him and waved from the queue.

"What did you have?"

"Hamburger. Fucking awful."

Norman lifted an index finger to his mouth and cocked his head as the distant tannoy crackled out the teams.

A crescendo of muffled boos reverberated along the corrugated iron roof of the shed as the West Ham team was announced.

"Moore's back for them...and Boyce in for Sissons at outside left. That's good news." Norman ran his finger down the programme line up and noted the changes.

"That means they're happy with a draw. Boyce will play more defensive." Scotty nodded and smiled at what he saw as positive news for Leeds.

The chatter in the queue paused as the announcer moved on to announce the home team, each name greeted with a loud cheer from the other side of the brickwork.

'1.Sprake, 2.Reaney, 3.Bell, 4.Bremner, 5. Charlton..'

"Yes, Jackie's back. He'll kick that fucking Byrne into the stand in the first five minutes..."

'6.Hunter, 7.Giles, 8.Storrie, 9.Peacock, 10.Collins, 11.Cooper.'

"Ah shit, no Jo-Jo again. Told you he was injured." Scotty turned to Norman.

"He's always fucking injured. I reckon it's the weather. Too cold for him here."

"Why where's he come from?" Alan had barely asked the question before Scotty and Norman burst into song in bad West Indian accents.

"Albert Johanneson, he's one of the few. I don't know where he comes from, I think it's Timbuktoo."

"Fucking hell." Alan shook his head as his friends laughed and the queue shuffled forward.

"Are we trying the boys turnstile, save 2/6 ?" Scotty stood on tiptoes as they passed the end of the stand wall and the clunk-click of the turnstiles got louder.

"No, the queue's bigger, let's just get in." Alan pushed him forward as a chant of 'Wembley here we come' began inside the ground and was quickly adopted by the queue outside.

"Need to win today lads!" An over-excited man in his late twenties, wearing a Leeds bobble hat shoved his way into the queue behind them, draping his arms over their shoulders and breathing recently supped beer into their faces.

"We can go top of the league today, and when we do, we're staying there...Come on Leeds!"

Chapter 42

"So you went in 'Popular Side then?" Scotty nudged
Wesley under the table in the Del Rio coffee bar, and his
friend slowly raised his head and rubbed at his eyes.

"Yeah, didn't get in till half seven this morning. Went
back to sleep after my alarm went off so I didn't get to
'ground till ten to three. Lowfields terrace was 'only place
I could get in."

"A point behind Chelsea with a game in hand, and seven
games to go. We just need to keep winning." Scotty
folded the Green Post and tossed it onto the table
between the empty coffee cups.

"Thank God for little Billy popping up with a winner
again today." Wesley picked up the paper and studied the
blurry front page picture of Alan Peacock scoring the
opening goal against West Ham.

Norman stood next to Non-Stop Nigel beside the pinball
table, occasionally glancing at the door to monitor the
early Saturday evening comings and goings.

"Looks like it's going to be busy tonight. The nice
weather's brought everyone out."

Four girls wearing ski pants and Hush Puppies fed the
juke box and 'My Guy' crackled from the single speaker.
A girl with a short bob signalled to Alan with a slight flick
of her lopsided fringe.

"Customers Norman...go sort them out." Alan remained
seated and Norman strolled across towards the girls,
whilst closely monitoring Luigi's movements behind the
counter.

Alan sipped at his coffee as he watched Norman furtively reach into his jacket pocket then push a brown envelope under the table and into a square vanity case held by one of the girls. Nigel grunted in frustration as the tilt light flashed on the pinball machine, and The Temptations replaced Mary Wells on the juke box. Wesley's attention remained fixed on the Green Post and he didn't look up as the door opened and three young men wearing Leeds scarves entered the café.

"Wes! We were just talking about you...just the man we wanted to see." Early twenties in a navy blue Harrington style jacket and unfaded Levi's, the young man's face was flushed pink after the two mile walk back from Elland Road. He approached the table as his two friends headed to the counter.

"Alright Stu...good result today eh?" Wesley spoke slowly and deliberately, but a sudden rapid tapping of his fingers on the table caught Alan's attention.

"Yeah, not the best game though. Peacock took his goal well, and what about that backheel from Jackie Charlton? Ace that wasn't it?" The young man smiled and flicked at a discarded napkin with the heel of his black brogues.

Wesley began to stand hesitantly, raising his hand slightly and mumbling inaudibly as the young man continued talking.

"Yeah, we wanted to talk to you about final tickets."

"Erm, well, it's not going to...let's go to the counter and I can tell you all..." Wesley nodded towards the other young men who were now heading back towards them.

"We were hoping you could sort us out again..." Stuart's words were lost as Wesley moved quickly to grab his arm and shove him away from the table, from where Alan and Scotty were now staring at them.

"Here he is...the man with the tokens!" The other youth had curly, copper coloured hair and was wearing a checked shirt and C&A cardigan, and he grinned as he stepped forward. "How much are you selling them for this time?"

"Alan don't..." Scotty reached out but couldn't stop Alan Connolly as he stood up and moved quickly towards Wesley, who raised a hand towards his mouth then turned slowly, before reeling backwards as Alan's fist connected with his jaw.

"You fucking stupid bastard! I told you! Get rid of the fucking things..." Wesley sprawled backwards across an empty table, then managed to regain his balance only to be floored again by a glancing blow to the temple, followed by a flurry of punches which despatched him onto the tea-stained linoleum. He curled in a ball, in anticipation of a continued assault, but instead heard the crash of crockery tumbling to the floor as Alan was restrained by Scotty and Non-stop Nigel.

"And you! You're another fucking traitor." Alan now directed his anger towards Scotty as a Nigel bear-hug pinned his arms to his sides.

"What did I do?" Scotty backed away until he reached the wall where he cowered, arms raised in front of him.

"I told you to get rid of the tokens with the van. So how has that cunt been selling them?"

"I don't know Alan, honestly, I burnt the bag in the van. He must have taken some out before. I don't know..."

"Boys! Stop! Enough. No fighting. Any fighting you must leave and you no come back here again." Luigi approached brandishing a dustpan and brush as the four girls helped Wesley to his feet.

"I'm sorry Wes. I didn't mean to drop you in it." Stuart stood back as Wesley rubbed at an egg-shaped lump appearing above his left eye.

"You're fucking finished son! Not only working for us, town is over for you. If I see you in here again, or at the BG, the Conc, the Coins...anywhere, then I fucking promise you..." Alan shook himself free of Nigel's grasp and reached into the lining of his suit.

"Alan no, leave it..." Norman stepped forward as Wesley began to back away at speed towards the door.

"I fucking promise you, if I see you around here again, I'll open your guts up." Alan smiled as he saw the other customers step back, the girls' eyes wide, Luigi jabbering about calling the police, Stuart and his friends shaking their heads, raising their hands, saying they don't want any trouble as he withdrew the bayonet from his jacket and pointed it at Wesley.

Switch flicked. Power current coursing from his brain and through his veins with an intensity that took his breath away. Take no prisoners. No fucking prisoners.

Chapter 43

The BG Club felt like a living entity, infused with an unstoppable chemical energy that propelled two hundred people to move in perpetual motion to the hypnotic groove of Booker T's Hammond organ, as Green Onions oozed like treacle from the speakers.

Alan leant on the counter, nodding in time to the music, failing to notice Elaine beside him until she tugged on the sleeve of his jacket.

"Where's Wes?" Her voice was barely audible but the words she mouthed were clear.

"Not here." Alan turned back to face the dancefloor.

"Well where is he? He said he'd meet me here."

"Fuck off Elaine."

Norman approached at speed from the cloakroom and moved to steer Elaine away.

"You're a shithead Alan, you know that?" Her voice raised now, but he pretended not to hear.

"No wonder Chrissie's gone to Moortown instead of here..."

Norman had taken hold of Elaine's arm and was leading her away from the counter when Alan pulled her back.

"Gone where?"

"She's gone to a party with her cousin. There's a lad there that fancies her, bit of an ace face so they say..."

"Where is it, the party?" Alan gripped her arm above the elbow. *Not mine, not yours.*

"Ow Alan, you're hurting...I don't know where, I think she said in the Talbots off Street Lane, I don't know the address."

Alan released his grip. "Norman, find Scotty and Nigel and get the scooters, we're going for a ride." *Switch flicked. Electricity crackling into life. Voices too loud to ignore.*

"What? I thought we had to shift all these pills tonight. Where are we going?" Norman looked from Alan back to Elaine who was pushing her way towards the dancefloor.

"Just get the scooters and I'll see you outside in five minutes." Alan caressed the bayonet in the lining of his jacket then reached into his top pocket and retrieved an envelope. He took a handful of half-pills and dropped them into his mouth while watching Elaine begin dancing with two lads in Fred Perry's and Harringtons.

"Sampling the product Alan?"

At first he thought it was fancy dress make-up. Four vertical lines, their appearance initiated by deep black scabs just above the eyebrow, descending in livid red stripes down Stanley Mortimer's left cheek.

"Christ, what happened to you?" Alan took a step back and regarded the face which resembled a house-of-horrors waxwork in the flashing lights. *Red, Green, Purple. Blood on his hands. Blood on his face.*

"Sapphire. Have you seen her?" Stanley raised a tentative hand to his face then retracted it and rubbed his fingers together.

"She did that?"

Stanley nodded and raised his polo neck to reveal heavy bruising on his ribs.

"And this. Attacked me with a hammer while I was asleep. Luckily she didn't go straight for my head. I took it off her but she still fought like a tiger for about half an hour."

"Why did she do that?"

"She's been more disturbed than usual these last couple of days. She says her shadow has returned again. She was ranting and raving about Gods and demons all night, then disappeared this morning. I thought she might have come here to see you." Stanley Mortimer scratched at a scab which dissected his left eyebrow.

"Me? No, why would she come to see me?"

"She has a thing about you old chap. I think she sees you as a kindred spirit. That you need to save each other, you know?"

"I don't fucking need saving Stanley. I think you need to take care of yourself pal, don't worry about me." Alan reached out and placed his hand on Stanley Mortimer's shoulder.

"I have to go. I'll put the word out though, ask the boys to keep an eye out for her."

Up the steps past the small stage with the DJ stand, the doorman nodded an acknowledgement as Alan passed and stepped onto the cobbles of White Horse Street. Turning right, he heard the rattle of the Lambrettas idling on Boar Lane and quickened his step towards the main road. He saw the parked Rover P5 before he saw the scooters, headlamps lit and a leather gloved hand beckoning through the open driver's side window.

"Father Ernest..." Alan spat out his gum and headed towards the car, exchanging glances with Norman and Scotty, parked twenty feet away. No words were spoken as Alan shuffled his feet nervously under the critical glare being directed at him from the driver's seat. Father Ernest turned away, looking through the windscreen and speaking slowly and gently, so that Alan needed to bend low towards him to catch the words.

"This isn't quiet."

"I beg your pardon?" Alan rested his hand on the door of the Rover as he leaned forward.

"You said town had been quiet. I've been to a few of your coffee bars. They aren't quiet. They're busy." Father Ernest tilted his head and raised his eyebrows to invite a response.

"You're right. It is busy tonight. Because the weather has warmed up. Much busier than it's been for weeks..." Norman revved his scooter and Scotty bent to check a misfiring exhaust, giving Alan an excuse to avoid eye contact with Father Ernest.

"So..." The priest tapped on the dashboard, looking through the windscreen towards the scooters.

"So, business is picking up. Should be a better night."

"Should be..." Ernest smirked and nodded gently.

"It will be. It will be a better night. We'll catch up on the pills. We'll shift all last weeks and this week's too." Alan didn't realise his hand was resting on the open window of the car until it was covered by Father Ernest's leather-gloved hand.

"Good. That's good." There was a long pause as Alan tried to remove his hand and Father Ernest tightened his grip.

"Remember Alan, keep your mind on business, instead of sin."

"Yes, I do. I will."

The priest removed his hand and Alan snatched back his own from the window.

"Make sure you do, because mark my words Alan, the stench of sin is all around you. Sin and lies. When did you last read the bible?"

"The bible? Erm...not sure, a few months ago maybe." Norman revved the Lambretta causing Alan to glance along Boar Lane.

"John Chapter 6, verse 64." Father Ernest straightened his gloves and looked at the scooters through the windscreen. Alan nodded, trying to disguise his confusion.

"You will do well to read and digest it. Consider how it applies to your current situation."

Father Ernest flicked at the indicator and glanced in the rear-view mirror, before turning the steering wheel and edging into Boar Lane, calling back towards the kerb as the Rover pulled away.

"Sin and lies, Alan...Sin, lies and betrayal."

Chapter 44

Turning left from Boar Lane, the two scooters headed up Briggate past Saturday night revellers enjoying the first signs that the Yorkshire winter was finally in retreat. Scotty with Nigel riding pillion lead the way, with Norman and Alan drawing level as they passed the Grand, heading out past the mock Tudor shopfronts of North Street, then up Chapeltown Road past the Polish Club and the Ukrainian supermarket, strains of blue beat from the streets running parallel with their blues clubs and shebeens. Another world, and not theirs.

Alan leant on the backrest, tilting his head towards the streetlights, feeling the weight of the bayonet in his jacket, the orange lamp glow alternating with the darkness of the sky. Orange and black, the electricity running through his veins. *Red, green, purple.*

Thoughts of Christine and Sapphire, Frankie fucking Fields and Clive Donovan. *Orange and black, electricity burning in his brain, humming, buzzing, getting louder.*

A priest in leather gloves and an old man wearing medals. *Red, green, purple.*

Squeezing the bayonet. Wesley, Elaine, Christine and a Moortown Jew boy . *Orange and black.*

Brylcream and beer, blood and gravel and a boy with a knife in his chest. *Blue eyes crying.*

"Whereabouts is it? Scotty pulled over at a bus stop next to the Queens Arms on Harrogate Road, its car park full of Anglias and Cortinas , the new middle classes of Chapel Allerton enjoying their weekend. *You've never had it so good.*

"Street Lane. Talbot something, she said."

Scotty nodded and pulled away from the kerb. Up the hill to the traffic lights next to the Cro-Magnon, the two scooters idling alongside each other, their multiple spotlights illuminating the back window of the car in front, cavalry on chrome horses. Scotty and Norman exchanged nervous glances. *Red. Orange. Green. Wired wrong, current fizzing, buzzing, deafening. Voices too loud to ignore.*

They turned into Street Lane, then right into Talbot Gardens, an avenue of post-war semis, neat gardens behind privet hedges, a small car in almost half the driveways, safe behind double gates. Left into Talbot Avenue, scanning the windows for telltale signs of life.

"This is daft, it could be anywhere." Norman muttered too loud to himself.

"Shut the fuck up, keep driving."

"Left or right?" The junction with Talbot Road opposite a school.

Alan didn't have to think. He knew. He could already feel it. *Electrical charge buzzing like a hive of bees in his head. White lights flashing. Orange, black, white.*

"Left."

They heard the music from a hundred yards away. Cilla Black's strangled vocals from the open windows of a half brick, pebble-dashed semi on the corner of East Moor Crescent. Twenty scooters filled the L-shaped pavement, following the curve of a well-tended hedge. Loud voices and the clink of glass became audible as the two scooters rattled to a halt and Scotty and Norman killed the engines.

177

Sudden, loud laughter from the garden made Alan's heart race. A male voice, too loud. Confident, challenging, mocking. Laughter again and the electricity in his brain surged. *Not mine, not yours. No prisoners. No fucking prisoners.*

 "Scotty, Norman, stay here. Nigel, you come with me." Alan stretched his leg to climb off the scooter, his right hand over the breast pocket of his suit jacket.

"And turn the engines back on." Alan pushed open the gate and stepped forward with Nigel lumbering in his wake.

The laughing man was stood alongside two other youths, facing two girls who were sitting on a garden bench clutching Babycham bottles. He was waving his arms and talking loudly, and wearing a burgundy shirt with white buttons, the top one fastened. *Fucking straight.*

He turned as Alan approached. He'd looked taller from a distance but close up he was more or less the same size, and Alan didn't even need to stretch for his forehead to connect with the boy's nose. He staggered backwards, eyes surprised wide as the girls stood, one screaming annoyingly, the other silent.

"What the fuck are you doing?" The first of the boy's friends was taller, maybe approaching six foot, and Alan's fist failed to register cleanly on his jaw, but he was still sent sprawling into the shrubbery.

"You want some too?" The third boy was already back-pedalling towards a rockery at the bottom of the garden.

"Didn't fucking think so...come on Nigel." Alan stepped towards the door where a girl was slumped, a pool of vomit splashed around her shoes on the step.

Into the hallway, a kid in a homemade t-shirt with lettering spelling 'USA' and 'YALE', swayed towards him and asked for a light.

"Fuck off." *Current in his head sparking and fizzing, body jolting in response to the surges of power. Voices too loud to ignore.*

Along the hallway, a girl in a knee length skirt and long black socks, pinprick pupils in wide white eyes smiling. Record changed with a long scratch, 'Be my Baby' crackling from a speaker in the room. *Lightning flashing, black clouds in his mind, storm rolling in.*

Into the kitchen, a table piled with bottles, a girl crying panda tears, kohl stripes down her cheek, a boy in a striped blazer stroking her hair. A group of lads staring. Nigel in the hallway shoving a boy in a polo neck back through the door. Cigarette smoke and vomit. Perfume and pill eyes. Shouts from the garden. *Current fizzing, lightning flaring, phosphorescent glare blinding now.*

Into the living room, bodies moving in the darkness, close, too close. Sweat and fear. *Be my little baby.*

Bottles smashing in the hall. A girl screaming. Pushing through the bodies, feet sticking to the carpet. *Red. Green. Purple. Storm breaking in his head.*

Through the bodies, pulling them apart. *Won't you say you love me.*

In the corner, arms around him, head on his shoulder. *I'll never let you go. Not yours, not mine.*

Lightning exploding in his brain. Hand in his jacket, out of his jacket. Silver flashing in the darkness. *Red. Green. Purple. Red. Red.*

Christine screaming, eyes wide. Cohen stumbling, eyes closed. *No prisoners. No fucking prisoners. Wired wrong.*

Chapter 45

Water filling his mouth. Water filling his nose. Tears filling his eyes.

Cold white tiles. Water on the tiles.

Cold Red tiles. Blood on the tiles.

Strong Arms. Safe now.

Blood on the tiles. Blood on the knife.

Blue eyes crying. Brown eye smiling.

Blue eyes crying. Green eye smiling.

Brown eye smiling, Green eye smiling.

Safe now wee man.

Chapter 46

Sunday 4 April 1965

He'd known it was bad, as soon as Norman's mother had shaken him awake on the settee to say there was someone at the door to see him. He knew as soon as he saw Terry Jackson's face. Knew from Terry's single word response to the question of how he'd found him at Norman's.

"Wesley." A single word and a nod towards the Ford Zodiac followed by a silent drive to the phone box at the bottom of Churwell Hill.

Now Alan was inches from Terry Jackson's unshaven face, the half open door of the phone box not offering enough ventilation to mask the smell of Saturday beer and cigarettes on his breath as he finally broke the silence.

"At least you had the sense to stay away from your flat. Coppers are waiting outside after your fuck up at that party last night. What's up with you?" *Wired wrong. Voices too loud to ignore.*

Alan shuffled his feet to try and stop his legs shaking as he listened to the second-hand ring tone from the receiver, followed by the shrill beep, whirr and clunk, as Jackson pushed a penny into the slot.

"Are you there? It's me...I've got him."

Alan heard no response before Terry passed him the receiver.

"Hello?" He looked at Terry and shrugged, hearing only muffled crackles down the line. "Hello, who is it?"

The silence was broken by a sound which caused the hairs on Alan's neck to bristle. A gasp... or maybe a stifled sob, followed by a low moan which morphed into a wail of terror which chilled his bones and made his heart pound in his chest.

"Keith...? Is that you?" Alan's words came out in a whisper and Terry Jackson turned away, unable to meet his horrified stare.

A tortured, unintelligible mumble, a bronchial, phlegm choked attempt at words, ended vainly in a succession of sobs.

"Keith, what's happening? Terry, what...?"

Terry Jackson took a deep breath and stepped from the phone box, shaking his head, looking at the ground.

The line went silent again and Alan stared at the receiver, his hand shaking.

"Alan." Clive Donovan's voice, so quiet that he almost missed it. "Are you there Alan?"

"Yes, I'm here. I don't understand..."

"Your chemist." The volume now increased, the words clear down the line.

"What? I don't know..."

"Don't insult my intelligence Alan. I know all about your side business and I also know about this new drug, this acid from America. And I want the man who knows how to make it."

Alan's stomach heaved, vomit stinging the back of his throat as he swallowed it and fought to control his breathing.

"Have you got Keith?" His breath came so fast he could hardly speak.

"Yes that's right. Your brother is spending some time with Father Ernest this morning. He's foregone his usual Sunday morning service for...a little dentistry. When the reverend opens his toolbox he really doesn't know when to stop you know."

"Don't hurt Keith, he knew nothing about it, I promise you. It was all me. I'll make it right, just don't hurt him."

"So you can bring me your chemist?"

"Yes, he's here in Leeds. Don't worry I'll bring him to you. Please, just stop..."

"You have an hour. Terry knows where."

The line clicked and buzzed and the sound didn't stop in his head when he put the receiver back in the cradle.

He pushed open the phone box door and Terry turned to face him, shaking his head.

"For fuck's sake kid, what have you done?"

"Where is he? Where have they got Keith?"

"At his flat. We went round first thing. Donovan hasn't slept all night. Smashed his cocktail cabinet up when he heard what you've been up to. You'd both be dead, you and Keith, but you're lucky..."

"Lucky? Jesus Christ...Who told him?" Alan ignored the dog shit and crouched on the grass verge, his head in his hands.

"Let's just say your pal Wesley had an impromptu confessional session with the priest. Anyway, Donovan's heard about this new acid drug. His pals in London are all talking about it. They reckon it's the next big thing, but no one knows how to make it. Your scientist is in demand and that's the only reason you and Keith are still alive."

"Will they definitely let Keith go if I take the chemist to them?" Alan looked up, seeking assurance, but Jackson stared away up Churwell Hill.

"I hope so kid, he's my mate, but I don't know what state he'll be in after the priest is done with him." He opened his mouth again but checked himself.

"Go on...you were going to say something." Alan stood up and Terry Jackson turned to face him.

"You though..." He shook his head. "What you've done, trying to con Donovan, that can't be undone even if you deliver your chemist."

"I know the score, but what choice do I have? He's my brother. He's all I've got." Alan walked towards the car. *Only we can see the demons.*

185

Chapter 47

"You'd better pray that he's here." Terry Jackson lowered his voice as they climbed the stairs to the second floor flat in Kensington Terrace. "I don't want to have to make that call if he's not Alan, I really don't."

"Don't worry, he will be. They stay in bed till late."

"What if he won't come?" Jackson paused for breath on the first floor landing.

"He has no choice." Alan raised his right hand and felt the weight of the bayonet in his jacket.

A noise from inside the flat caused Alan to pause and press his ear to the door. *Mr Tambourine man playing a song for me.*

"Sounds like they're up anyway." He turned the handle and pushed open the door, peering round the frame into the living room.

"Stanley? Are you there?"

They stepped forward along the narrow hallway, Terry Jackson pausing to examine a statue of a six-armed god.

"Stanley...It's me, Alan."

He walked over to the record player and watched the black vinyl revolving, before pulling back the curtains to look out at the three storey red brick terrace opposite.

"Who are you?" Sapphire emerged from the kitchen, naked and clutching a large kitchen knife, her gaze fixed on Terry Jackson who was running a finger along the contents of a bulging bookcase.

"Sapphire...this is Terry. He's with me. Where's Stanley?"

She turned and noticed Alan for the first time.

"I knew you'd come. Mara sent Namuci to bring you to me." She smiled as she approached, wrapping her arms around him, the hilt of the knife pressing hard into his back as her lips met his, her tongue probing his mouth.

"Come on, let's screw." She took his hand and pulled him in the direction of the bedroom as Alan made eye contact with Terry Jackson and shrugged.

"No, Sapphire, I need to speak with Stanley. It's urgent." Alan stopped and pulled his hand free.

"Stanley's gone..." She brushed her hair from her face and tapped the knife blade gently on her lower lip.

"Gone? Gone where? I only saw him last night...he didn't say anything about leaving?" *Fuck.Fuck.Fuck. Switch flicked, electrical current fizzing into life.*

"Well, he didn't know. Neither of us did. Then Mara came in a dream and told me Stanley had to leave. Turns out it was him who was drawing my shadow back all along. Crazy huh?"

"So where is he now?" Alan's mouth was so dry he found himself unable to swallow.

Sapphire smiled and tossed her hair and span across the room in time to the music.

"He flew away. He's free now. I can show you what he left behind though, he doesn't need it anymore." She led the way towards the bedroom and pushed open the door. Terry Jackson was the first to peer around the door frame, then recoil, ashen faced, his hand to his mouth.

"Jesus Christ..."

Sapphire stepped back, a gentle smile lighting up her face as Jackson pushed past her. Alan paused, watching Terry stagger towards the door, Sapphire giggling as she entered the bedroom.

"Come on Alan, come and see!" The bedsprings squeaked and he forced himself to slowly open the door, to see Sapphire bouncing playfully on the bed, smiling back at him, cradling Stanley Mortimer's head, lifting it from the pillow, kissing his white lips just as passionately as she had Alan's a moment earlier.

Alan became aware of a noise, a low moan of distress and realised it was coming from deep within himself as he staggered backwards to rest against the wall, his gaze fixed on the decapitated body lying before him on the bedroom floor.

"You see Alan, Stanley wasn't like me and you. His ego was tied to his earthly self. He attracted shadows. Mara told me I had to set him free." Sapphire playfully ruffled Stanley Mortimer's hair and gazed into his unseeing eyes as she rested his head beside her own on the blood-soaked pillow.

"His ego is free now Alan. It's time for us to join him, come on, come to bed and let's fly together." She tapped the mattress with a blood soaked hand and teased her nipples erect with the knife blade.

"Fuck...no...you don't know what you've done. You've killed him. You've killed me." *The switch flicked off, current disconnected, power drained, lights out. Forever.*

Chapter 48

Alan Connolly rested a hand on the wall on either side of the narrow staircase as he descended at speed towards the open door, gasping for air as he made it to the three external steps leading to a weed strewn front garden.

Terry Jackson was bent double next to the Zodiac, blowing snot and vomit from his nostrils, turning to look at Alan as he sank down onto the top step. The sound of glass smashing and Sapphire crying or laughing or laughing and crying echoed down from the second floor but his legs were shaking so much he was unable to move.

"Alan, we need to get out of here, come on mate." Jackson leant on the gate and cast a wary eye towards the second floor window.

"What happens now?" Alan tried to stand but his head span uncontrollably.

Terry Jackson shook his head and turned away.

"Fuck knows...this is bad, really bad."

Alan slowly made his way down the garden path and climbed into the passenger seat without looking back at the house.

Terry Jackson fired the ignition and crunched the Ford into gear and slowly pulled away from the kerb in silence. A fat black woman in a head scarf with a toddler in a pushchair stared as the wheels screeched into a left turn on Hyde Park Road.

"What happens now Terry? What are you going to say to Donovan?" Alan stared ahead through the windscreen but received no response. Terry Jackson breathed heavily and pushed the accelerator hard to the floor, barely braking before swerving left in front of the church at the junction with Hyde Park Terrace.

He turned the key in the ignition to kill the engine and both men stared in silence at the red telephone box on the corner of the street in front of them.

Alan opened his mouth but Terry Jackson answered his question before he'd uttered the words.

"I don't know Alan. I don't fucking know."

Chapter 49

"Are you sure about this?"

Alan Connolly's hand was shaking so much he could barely hold the receiver in the phone box on Hyde Park Terrace.

Terry Jackson nodded and closed his eyes as Alan stretched the cord to it its full length, then brought the receiver down hard just above his right eyebrow.

"Fuck...Bastard!" Terry Jackson recoiled and covered his face with his hands.

"Sorry Terry but you said to do it hard."

"Yeah, yeah...it needs to look good. Fuck..." Terry lowered his hands and blood poured from a gash in a large swelling above his eye.

"Have you got a hanky or summat?"

"No, sorry. It certainly looks good though." Alan leant back to examine the wound as the swelling increased and Jackson's eye began to close.

"You're going to have to be quick. I'll say you whacked me in the flat and took the keys and I couldn't find a phone box, but owt beyond half an hour they'll get suspicious. You do know how to drive don't you?" Jackson handed Alan the Zodiac keys.

"Aye, course. Nicked my first car at thirteen."

"What are you going to do? If this goes wrong, I'm going to end up in the same hole as you and your kid on Ilkley Moor."

"I'll knock on the door and hopefully the priest will answer. I'll do him straight off with the bayonet. You sure Donovan won't be armed?"

"No, he never carries. Leaves it to Ernest. There was only the two of them when I left, hopefully they haven't brought any of the other lads in."

"Well, if they have, I'll just have to deal with them too." *Current surging, charge exploding in his head. No fucking prisoners.*

Terry Jackson looked down at his blood-soaked hands through one eye.

"I know Keith's your brother Alan but he's my best mate too. I wouldn't take this risk for anyone else. Don't fuck this up or all three of us will die in the worst way possible." *Tick Tock.*

Chapter 50

Pushing sixty on two wheels through red lights at Hyde Park corner. Seventy past the feast on Woodhouse Moor, pikey kids squatting by the roadside, shitting on cinders. Eighty, wrong side of the road passing a milk float opposite the university.

Lightning flashing in his mind, the script taking shape in his head. *The knock on the blue door. Inside the flat,an exchange of glances. 'That'll be Terry with the chemist.' Ernest putting down the plyers. Donovan smiling, feet in blood. Door lock rattling. Blue door, turning red. Alan waiting. Alan hating. The blade in his hands. The surprise in his eyes. The blade in his neck. Blood on the walls. Down the hall. Donovan standing, Donovan falling. Feet in blood. Keith smiling. Safe now.*

Then what? Then what. *Ideas and bravery. Sin and lies.*

Woodhouse Lane, the Merrion Centre, a vision of the future, shopping without cars and rain. *One hundred miles an hour. Red. Green. Purple.*

Headrow, Vicar Lane, New York Street and the smell of death and cow shit. *Two hundred miles an hour. Lightning flashing in his mind.*

Past the bus station, a blur of two tone green. Quarry Hill's grey ramparts. Millgarth close enough for a quick piss for the two men in the black Ford Anglia parked outside the flats. One asleep, trilby over his eyes. Double time making up for a night in a car park. Not seeing him, not expecting the Zodiac.

Two hundred yards away. Turning off the engine and winding down the window. Leaning in, hand on the horn. *Now you see me. What I am. Who I am.*

Off and running into the block, looking back, trilby man rubbing his eyes, his mate twenty feet behind. Up the stairs and along the landing, panting as he reached the door, electrical current coursing through his veins, sparking in his mind, hammering on the door. *Not mine, not yours. Ideas and bravery. Two hundred miles an hour. No fucking prisoners.*

Chapter 51

As he'd expected, it was the priest who opened the door, taking a step back and quickly reaching inside his jacket with a crimson hand, fumbling to remove the Webley revolver from an inside pocket.

Alan looked to the left, hearing the bang of the landing door, the footsteps on the stairs, then back to Father Ernest.

"Not going to ask me in then, you cunt?"

"Put it down now! Put down the gun!" The priest turned on hearing the voice, to see Trilby Man advancing along the landing, arms extended, palms facing down, as his red faced colleague nervously peered round the wall corner.

"What the fuck have you done?" Ernest narrowed his eyes as Alan smiled back at him. Taking a backward step, the priest tried to close the door but Alan's desert boot got there first, and with a heave of his shoulder he was in, moving down the narrow hallway of the flat, Father Ernest backing away towards the living room, levelling the pistol at his forehead. *Black static crackling and exploding in his head, white light flashing in his eyes. Now you see me, you cunt.*

Clive Donovan appeared in the doorway, mouth open, exposing brown teeth and yellow tongue, eyes flashing with surprise and rage as Father Ernest backed towards him, followed by Alan Connolly extending a Japanese bayonet in his right hand. Behind them, the face of a middle-aged man wearing a trilby hat peered nervously round the doorframe and into the hallway.

"Oh Alan, what have you done?" Clive Donovan stepped back into the room, to stand beside the centrally positioned dining chair, upon which Keith Connolly slumped, face down, his chin resting on a white shirt turned red. Two bloodied masses, the remains of his ears, lay on the carpet on either side of his stockinged feet, alongside a hand's worth of mismatched fingers.

It smelled of fear and blood and shit and now the black electricity wasn't only fizzing in his head, it filled the whole room and the circuit connected the four of them – Father Ernest, breathing heavily, nostrils flaring, his arm extended, red hand steady as it pointed the heavy, black revolver; Clive Donovan, licking at his lips, bulbous tongue rolling across tar-stained teeth, left arm gently stroking Keith Connolly's blood-matted hair; Keith, eyes swollen shut, nostrils crusted black above a mouth destroyed by the pilers laying at his feet amidst a carpet of teeth.

"It's over. You're finished." Alan stepped forward, the tip of the bayonet inches from the barrel of the gun.

"And so are you..." Clive Donovan looked beyond Alan at the two men in suits and raincoats advancing cautiously along the hallway, truncheons drawn.

"Put the gun down Ernest. Half of Millgarth is running across the road as we speak. Give it up." The first detective stepped into the room behind Alan.

"When I've told them all about your business, you won't be getting out until you're a very old man. I'll still be young." Alan dropped the bayonet and raised his hands.

"But you won't be getting out. You think I don't have influence in Armley?" Donovan gently stroked Keith's head and smiled as Father Ernest lowered the gun.

"All three of you, on your knees, facing the wall, hands behind your backs."

Alan felt a shove from behind as more officers entered the room and he was pushed against the wall.

"That's my brother, I need to see him."

"Alan Connolly, I'm arresting you for malicious wounding, grievous bodily harm, possession of a controlled substance with intent to supply, extortion..." Alan felt his arms being pulled behind his back and the cold metal of the handcuffs cut into his wrists.

"And if I have my way, we'll also be adding the murder of Horace Wilson to that list." The face of the man in the trilby appeared inches from his own and he smelt stale tobacco, flask coffee and a night in a car park.

"Sergeant, have you called for an ambulance, this one is in a bad way."

"Is he alive? Please...he's my brother." Alan was forced to his knees facing the wall alongside Clive Donovan and Father Ernest.

"I thought you Scotch lads were meant to be tough...he cried like a baby when the vicar opened his toolbox. Isn't that right Ernest?" Clive Donovan's hissed words from three feet away caused Alan to breath hard, straining against the handcuffs which restrained him.

Alan sensed the fake priest turning towards him but carried on staring straight ahead at the flock wallpaper.

"John Chapter 6, verse 64. You didn't read it did you?"

"What the fuck are you talking about?"

"Yet there are some who do not believe, who would betray you...You lost a member of your flock Alan. It was young Wesley who told us about your sideline."

"Fucking Wesley... no ambition, no plan. It doesn't matter though, time is on my side, not yours. Everything you two have worked for, all these years. Everything you've earned. It's gone. It's all going to be mine. You can think about that while you rot away in a jail cell for the rest of your lives." *Only we can see the demons.*

"Keep facing the wall!" The detective in the trilby bent to growl into his ear, and Alan turned his head in response to a heavy, bronchial splutter as more officers arrived and untied Keith and laid him on the carpet. Struggling to hear what was being said, their hushed, urgent tones caused a knot to tighten in his stomach. *Fuck.Fuck.Fuck.*

Clive Donovan and Father Ernest were hauled to a standing position and led from the flat, but Alan was left facing the wall.

"What's happening?"

More voices entered the room and he heard the sound of medical equipment being unpacked, catching only snatches of the conversation. *Blood loss. Multiple lacerations. Amputation. Drugs. Prolonged torture. Brother. His brother.*

A hand on his shoulder caused Alan to shiver.

"We have to go. You can see him for a minute. It's...not looking good. One minute, that's all."

Chapter 52

"It's me brother. I'm here."

"Alan." Eyelashes sealed closed by a thick glue of dried blood parted to reveal a brown iris amidst a swelling of purple flesh.

"Aye, I'm here Keith. It's going to be okay." *Safe now.*

An ambulanceman bent down alongside Alan and dabbed tentatively at the gaping crimson maw which was Keith's mouth, causing him to gasp and inhale deeply.

"They're going to take you to hospital. It's going to be alright Keith." Alan fought back tears as he sensed the presence of the detective stood over him, feeling a knee in his back as he crouched, handcuffed beside his brother, his feet crunching teeth. *Blood on the carpet. Tears in his eyes.*

The ambulanceman soaked the cloth in water from a metal jerry can and gently wiped Keith's left eye. Unspoken words rasped in his throat as he struggled to clear blood from his larynx, and he blinked slowly to reveal a bloodshot green iris amidst a swelling of red flesh.

Brown eye crying, Green eye crying.

"Your eyes....they're different colours. I forgot."

Alan gasped for breath, feeling like he'd been punched in the chest. *Tears in their eyes. Their eyes brown and green.*

"That day...."

"Aye..that day." Keith's words were barely audible, less than a whisper, his words ill-formed and distorted following the removal of his lower lip.

Strong arms. Safe now wee man..

"You...it was you that saved me." Alan shaking his head, trying to remember. Wanting to forget.

Keith closed his eyes again. *Brown and green.* A blood-tainted tear edged its way along the skin folds beneath his eye and trickled down his cheek. *Brown eye crying, Green eye crying.*

"Me..."

"It was you...you that saved me...you...you that killed ma." *Electric shocks in his brain. Lightning flashing white, scorching holes in his memory, igniting his brain, burning it all down.*

"It's time to go." The knee pushed harder into his back.

"I had to... she would have killed you..." *You're killing the boy.*

"No...it's not true." *Why do you make me do it.*

"In here lads...have you got the oxygen?" The ambulanceman turned as his colleagues manhandled a clanking metal gurney into the hallway.

"Come on, I said one minute." Knee in his back, a hand on his shoulder.

"But Da...?" Alan leant in, his face close to Keith's. *Stubble kisses. Sweat and tobacco. Brylcream and beer.*

"Wasn't there...took the blame for me. Went down.. to save me." *Why do you make me do it.*

"Up...on your feet." The hand under his arm, trying to lift him, Alan still leaning forward, trying to catch the words.

"Don't be scared Alan...of being him." *Pencil in his neck. Blood on his hands.*

"I'm putting this mask on you now son, giving you something to ease the pain."

The ambulanceman turned to Alan. "Say goodbye to your brother, we're taking him to Jimmy's. You can see him there."

The detective failed to stifle a laugh, hauling Alan to his feet as the ambulance crew grunted and strained and hauled Keith onto the gurney.

"I very much doubt that pal. This lad is going straight to the Bridewell, then to Armley, for a long, long time."

Alan leant forward, staring hard into his brother's unblinking eyes, one brown one green, searching for answers to questions he couldn't bear to ask. *Blood on his hands.*

"I'm sorry Alan... It's over now." Keith closed his eyes and the oxygen mask filled with condensation as he spoke.

Alan watched as the ambulance crew raised the sides of the gurney and began to manoeuvre it through the door into the hallway of the flat. He felt the detective's grip on his upper arm, steering him towards the door, following the ambulancemen.

The narrow hallway was filled with dark overcoats and the smell of antiseptic, clanking medical equipment and crackling radios as the ambulance crew debated the best way to get the gurney out of the door. Keith reached out his hand and Alan's arm moved instinctively, forgetting the handcuffs which restrained him.

"I'm still here."

Keith's eyes flickered fearfully, and he gasped into the mask, his gaze scanning the faces above him before making eye contact with his brother.

"Don't be scared anymore ..."

The detective tightened his grip on Alan's arm and attempted to steer him past the stretcher.

"Come on, move."

Alan held Keith's stare as he edged past, and the oxygen mask filled with blood and snot as his brother struggled to speak.

"Don't be scared...he wasn't the monster."

The gurgled words, distorted by mucous and congealed blood, were only half heard as Alan reached the door, causing him to pause, leaning back to face his brother as the detective pushed him forward. Struggling against the man holding him and the handcuffs restraining him, he turned his head, shouting back into the hallway as he was manhandled through the doorway.

"But he was brother, he was the monster, but I'm not scared of the monster anymore... because I've become one myself."

"Shut up and keep walking." A punch in the kidneys from the detective propelled him through the door and Alan Connolly laughed and looked out across St. Peter's Street towards Millgarth, with the grey sky turning black above the market.

"I'll see you again brother, maybe here, maybe in another place, but believe me this isn't the end for Alan Connolly. In fact, I've got a feeling this is just the beginning."

Epilogue

Leeds United's quest for a league and cup double in their first season back in England's top flight would ultimately end in failure. A league schedule of 8 games in 23 days in April 1965 saw Leeds concede the title to Manchester United on goal average. Their points tally of 61 would have made them champions in all but three of the seasons after World War 2, and they lost the title by a margin of 0.686 of a goal. In the FA Cup final against Liverpool on May 1st, Revie's exhausted team succumbed to an 81st minute goal, to lose the game 2-1. They had to wait another 3 years to secure their first major honour with a league cup final victory over Arsenal in 1968, which was followed by a first league title in 1969. From that year, there followed a golden period in which the team never finished outside the top 3 before winning a second league title in 1974. They also won two UEFA Fairs cup finals and the FA Cup in 1972, before Revie departed in 1974 to manage England, and the 'Super Leeds' era drew to a close.

Edwin (Eddie) Gray, Peter Lorimer and Jimmy Greenhoff – After making his Leeds debut as a 15 year old in 1962, Lorimer had to wait until the 1965-66 season to cement his place in the first team, with Gray making his breakthrough the following season. Both became legends of the game, between them making 1200 appearances for United and both winning international caps for Scotland. Gray also went on to manage Leeds twice, and in 2000 was voted the 3rd greatest player of all time at the club. Jimmy Greenhoff played over 100 games for Leeds after making his debut in 1963 before being transferred to Birmingham in 1968. He later went to Manchester United where he won an FA Cup winners medal in 1977 when he deflected home the winning goal.

Clive Donovan – Served 11 years of a 16 year sentence for racketeering and was released from prison on the grounds of ill health in 1977. Became a founder member of the 'Friday Morning breakfast club' with his friend Jimmy Savile. He died in 1989 at the age of 79.

Father Ernest – Returned to his theological studies while serving an 18 year sentence in Wakefield prison. He was ordained as a priest at HMP Kirkham in 1978 and was paroled in 1980. He undertook a role as a church sexton in a small village in the Lake District until his death in 1990 at the age of 75.

Terry Jackson – After serving a five year sentence for extortion, he returned to Harehills where he lived with his wife and son Max. He served two further jail terms for handling stolen goods, before becoming landlord of the Waterloo pub in 1982, where he remained until his death from a heart attack in 1987, aged 54.

Norman Cowell – Served a 2 year sentence for extortion and supply of a controlled substance. Became one of the pioneers of the skinhead scene in Leeds and opened a reggae record shop in Harehills in 1970. In 1975 he ran the first white-owned blues club in Francis Street, and became a community spokesman during the 1981 riots. Served as a local councillor until his retirement in 2012. He still lives in Chapeltown where he is a respected elder in the Rastafarian community.

Brian 'Scotty' Scott – Completed an apprenticeship in automotive mechanics at HMP Wetherby and worked as a mechanic in Leeds upon his release, before acquiring joint ownership of a garage business in East End Park in 1985 where he worked until his retirement in 2017 at the age of 70.

Wesley Smith – Received a suspended sentence after giving evidence for the prosecution in the trials of Clive

Donovan and his business associates. Left Leeds in late 1965, living in Scotland and London, before emigrating to Australia. Set up the Kalgoorlie branch of the Leeds United supporters club in 1990 and his ambition is to see another Leeds game in his lifetime. His last visit to Elland Road was the 2-1 win against West Ham on 3 April 1965.

'Non-Stop' Nigel Derry- Yorkshire and Humberside pinball champion 1966,1967,1969. Worked as a bodyguard to Peter Stringfellow and was head doorman at Cinderella's Rockafella's from 1972 to 1976. Died of a heart attack in Winchester Prison, aged 48 in 1991.

Christine Harrison – Gave birth to a son, Neil, in December 1965 at the age of 18. Married Dennis Yardsley in 1968 and had another son, Stuart in 1971. Continued to work at Woolworths until retiring due to ill health in 1986. Died of smoking related emphysema in 1991.

Sapphire - Police investigating the murder of Stanley Mortimer failed to trace the woman known as Sapphire. A search of the Hyde Park flat yielded only a California State driving licence in the name of Susan Denise Atkins. They failed to locate the owner of the licence and the murder of Stanley Mortimer remains unsolved.

Keith Connolly – Spent the first year of a six year jail sentence in the hospital wing of HMP Leeds, where he underwent numerous unsuccessful facial reconstruction surgeries. Transferred to Rampton high security hospital in 1967, he was diagnosed with paranoid schizophrenia and manic depression. He died in 1972 aged 32. The cause of his death was not disclosed.

Alan Connolly – Alan Connolly...well.. that's another story.

More books by Billy Morris available in all Amazon stores–

Bournemouth 90

It's April 1990 and the world is changing. Margaret Thatcher clings to power in the face of poll tax protests, prison riots and sectarian violence in Northern Ireland. The Berlin wall has fallen, South Africa's Apartheid government is crumbling and in the Middle East Saddam Hussein is flexing his muscles, while Iran is still trying to behead Salman Rushdie. In Leeds, United are closing in on a long-awaited return to the first division. Neil Yardsley is heading home after three years away and hoping to go straight. That's the plan, but Neil finds himself being drawn back into a world of football violence and finds a brother up to his neck in the drug culture of the rave scene. Dark family secrets bubble to the surface as Neil tries to help his brother dodge a gangland death sentence, while struggling to keep his own head above water in a city that no longer feels like home. The pressure is building with all roads leading to the south coast, and a final reckoning on a red-hot Bank Holiday weekend in Bournemouth that no one will ever forget.

Amazon Reviews of Bournemouth 90-

"Fast paced unflinching read."

"Well researched, 'in the know' story."

"Earthy, Leeds-based, Guy Ritchie style underworld thriller."

"The timeline & atmosphere around the build-up and description of that weekend captures just what it was like to be there."

LS92

Two years have passed, but the events of Bournemouth 90 continue to cast a dark shadow over the lives of everyone who travelled south on that hot Bank Holiday weekend. Max Jackson is out of jail and trying to re-establish himself in a Leeds underworld being torn apart by gangland warfare. The Yardsley brothers are still paying the price for their actions, with the spectre of Alan Connolly continuing to haunt them. At Millgarth, Sergeant Andy Barton finds himself in the limelight after Bournemouth, but terrace culture is changing, and police intelligence is struggling to adapt to the new normal of the nineties. At Elland Road, a resurgent United are heading towards their first league title in eighteen years, but a disturbing, malevolent force is threatening to gatecrash the champions' victory party. Old scores are settled and new ones imagined, as the climax to the title showdown becomes a deadly quest for vengeance, forgiveness and redemption. LS92. Dark crime fiction from a time when it was still grim up north.

Amazon Reviews of LS92-

" Fast moving crime thriller which picks up the pace two years on from Bournemouth 90, and captures the changing skyline of 1992 inner city Leeds, with its unforgiving streets, dubious bars and the unique characters of its time."

"If you like crime thrillers with a touch of terrace culture you will enjoy the journey this book takes you on."

"What can you say about a book that you read cover to cover in one session? There's almost no higher praise than that."

Birdsong on Holbeck Moor

Autumn 1918. The Great War is drawing to an end and the troops are coming home. The Leeds Pals who survived the carnage of the Somme are returning to a city in the grip of a deadly pandemic, food rationing and unemployment.
In Armley, a war hero needs one more big score to settle a crippling underworld debt, but his illicit wartime schemes are over and time is running out for Frank Holleran and his family. Wartime champions Leeds City FC find themselves in the eye of a financial storm and struggle to remain a footballing force as the full league resumes. Sports reporter Edgar Rowley is diverted from Elland Road to track an occult animal killer, while helping his brother to overcome his battlefield demons.1919 is set to be a momentous year, but for some in Leeds, the consequences of their past actions will mean that it's never going to be peaceful. Dark, World War 1 crime fiction from the year that the City became United.

Amazon Reviews of Birdsong on Holbeck Moor-

"Refreshingly different- dark, fast-paced, with short, snappy chapters that allow the story to flow from many different perspectives."

"Thoroughly researched and well written"

"As ever the writing is tight within this book and Morris manages to juggle the various plotlines effectively."

"There are heroes and villains in this book but not in the clichéd way you find in other crime novels."

"For those that know the Leeds story - and that we've been cursed for years...then this is where our soul begins, the first stamp of our DNA."